Full
CIRCLE

Kay Rogal
author of *Sweet Revenge*

CRIMSON
ROMANCE
F+W Media, Inc.

Published by
Crimson Romance
an imprint of F+W Media, Inc.
10151 Carver Road, Suite 200
Blue Ash, Ohio 45242

www.crimsonromance.com

ISBN 10: 1-4405-5719-5
ISBN 13: 978-1-4405-5719-4
eISBN 10:1-440-5720-9
eISBN 13:978-1-405-5720-0

Dedication

For my son, Seth. You inspire me to be creative. To Jennifer and Julie—thank you for allowing me the chance to make this fly higher than its original form and for making it fun.

To my readers and Seth, we all have a journey to travel. May we always find something to advocate for, smile, and laugh along the way. Reach high for your dreams—no matter how many obstacles get in the way. You will succeed!

Prologue

"You can't interfere with destiny," the three white orbs floating into the darkened room warned simultaneously. "It's not as if we don't empathize, but if we open our portal for just one minute, it's that *one* minute that may exterminate us all. Isn't it better to jeopardize one person in order to save many souls?"

Marion ignored them for the moment, halting the floating images with a single sweep of her hand, understanding all too well the implications of what she was about to do. She glanced up at the sky window and rubbed her hands over her arms to ward off the chill as the black haze hovered in the moonlight.

The black haze was Council's trail seeker.

A bloodhound.

Even though the black haze could not detect them through the cloaking shield, she could not stop past memories of Council's painful wrath entering her mind. The original Council members, visionaries of a better world, had been killed and replaced by those wanting power over peace. There were many souls still willing to defy the new Council, choosing to mutiny and scatter to Earth until a new world could be created to protect their souls from a fate worse than death.

Permanent extinction.

When Council learned the mutineers had disappeared and created a renegade world, they were furious, creating devastation wherever they could to draw Lake Hope out in the open in exchange for saving massive lives.

"It's a chance we'll have to take. If we don't go after her..." Marion glanced at her sister, Esther, before eyeing the black haze. Every hint of magic used provided a link in bringing Council closer in destroying them. "It will not end well."

Esther's recent vision had revealed the girl's powers had not surfaced and showed the source with the power to unleash them. That person was their nephew, Dante—the only one who may be able to save their world and Earth.

What do you do to find and convince a man, listed as one of the hundred most powerful of their world and Earth, to acknowledge the existence of his heritage and the duty bound to it for eternity?

Whatever it takes.

Even if it means evoking his wrath.

Esther had received word from Council's personal seer; Council knew of this girl's power and had vowed to stop at nothing to get it, to the point of commissioning Jack the Ripper's soul to find her.

"Have you located the girl?" Esther asked.

As Marion waved her hand towards the sky window, the glass parted. "She doesn't know of the worlds existing outside of her Earth. It takes time to find the right place to reveal our community without raising suspicion." She sighed. Sometimes older sisters had no patience. "They have their ways in finding what they want. You know, Esther, there's a reason why you haven't married," Marion joked, trying to find something to smile about.

"I was born a Steele and will leave this world as a Steele," Esther remarked with tartness.

Marion spared a quick glance over her shoulder as she flipped her silver braid over her shoulder. "Stop pacing," she told Esther, her own patience skating a fine line.

Turning back to the frozen images, Marion swept her hands apart to enlarge the floating images in front of her. Eye strain was no longer an issue, thanks to her old friend, Jeremiah Downey, who had refused to join them, staying on the run—but not before he tapped into the main virtual reality link.

"It isn't time. When it is, I will find you. Right now, the longer I stay, the easier it will be for Council to find you. There's a leak on your side. Until it's found, Council will always be one step behind," Jeremiah had said.

Finally Marion couldn't take Esther's pacing any longer. "Would you please sit down. You. Are. Driving. Me. Nuts."

Esther stopped, hands on ample hips, brows raised, ignoring the whispering and the other twenty sets of eyes in the room. "What would you have me do? Lean over your shoulder?" Esther winked with a wicked gleam at Marion's sisterly frustration. "I didn't think so. You do your thing. I'll do mine." Esther's backless heels resumed pacing, flopping with small thuds on the artificial grass.

It was difficult for Marion to concentrate with Esther's thoughts seeping into hers. Although Esther's wall prevented anyone from reading her mind, their blood ties meant she couldn't stop the overflow of horrors Council could inflict if they were caught. *Stop worrying so much,* Esther's telepathic message came through loud and clear to Marion, reverting to the form of communication their family been born with.

Do we not have the power to provide obstacles? Esther asked, blocking out the conversation around them.

"Dante's been located," Marion said.

The noise in the room died an instant death.

Esther squinted over her wire rim glasses, focused on the images in the air. She opened her mind to everyone in the room. *Someone please turn up the light.*

The stars shimmered slightly.

Esther caught the elderly Sarah Water's movements, grateful Sarah had pulled this spell off without a hitch. *Thank you, Sarah.*

Suddenly the stars shimmered into a blinding brightness.

Esther shielded her eyes. She had spoken too soon.

Marion raised her index finger in the air, and with a quick twist of the wrist, the stars dimmed to a soft glow.

"FYI," Marion announced over her shoulder. "The white explosion just blind-sided the poor pilot and he is now en-route to the hospital. He's okay, but Dante is hotter than an iron poker sitting in a bed of coals. He knows we've found him and doesn't like being controlled." She gave the eighty-three-year-old Sarah a gentle smile over her shoulder, "We've created another national stir and let's pray Council hasn't received another lead. At least this time we were able to bring this one back a little sooner."

Soon it may be all over.

Not a single person in the room staked a claim to the silent words.

No one needed to.

Chapter One

Dante Steele paced in his office. There was something wrong and he didn't like it. The only person powerful enough to touch his mind was Aunt Esther. For the last fortnight, he had awakened every night to someone trying to breach past his mind barrier in an effort to track him down.

He wanted no part of his past or heritage.

It had only brought devastation into his life, killing two people he loved most.

The day he obtained complete control of his powers, he had left without looking back.

When his pilot became blindsided by the light of the stars, he knew he had been found. He had never thought they would send a general tracking probe spiraling into the unknown, bouncing off human minds, searching for images or an energy trail of his existence.

Or sucked into a void there was no escaping.

There was only one way to end it.

He unbuttoned his suit as he waited for his secretary to answer the intercom. After he instructed her to take the next two weeks off with pay, he disconnected the intercom and took off his coat, laying it over the arm of the chair. He had already arranged her severance pay and letter of recommendation, knowing he would never come back here. Using his sight at this moment was a convenience to ensure his secretary had left the building. After darkening the windows and locking the doors, he stood in the middle room.

This room, this building, conveyed power and wealth of great magnitude on Earth. Compared to his world it was an ordinary life. One that did not include friends or lovers, because if his past erupted past the barrier he had erected, he was not sure he would make another century with more death on his conscience.

Now hell was on his heels, whispering to ignore the wake of its wrath or dare to follow.

If hell had the balls to dare him, he would not disappoint.

He tracked each link to the depths of darkness. Piece by piece, he slowly demolished the erected barriers until a small opening emerged. Tiny fissions of light reached out, yearning to be released from their prison. The darkness was holding it prisoner, threatening that there was no returning if he took back what he had forsaken.

All these years, he had hidden from his past. From life. His heritage. The knowledge that was now mocking him for not remembering that if he forsook his power too long, it would destroy him.

For him, there was no other choice.

It was either kill or be killed.

He did not hesitate and reached in, yanking the past, and hell, back.

Darkness and light fought, neither willing to surrender.

His soul waited patiently as if it had known there was no refusing what the past hid. Light reached out for an anchor, overpowering the darkness in an effort to be free.

His hand surrounded the source of the light and offered it to his soul, shielding the pent up power from leaking to unknown sources waiting to destroy their kind.

His soul greedily accepted the power, soaking all that it was fed.

As the seal of his soul sheathed the power, he released his hands, knowing it wouldn't be long.

There was always a price to pay for forsaking one's soul of its heritage.

Lightning flashed through his mind, rippling, arcing with a vengeance through his body. Every muscle contorted with a hell he had never experienced, never imagined. It was worse than when he had lost those he loved.

This was a different kind of hell.

A forewarning of a new hell to come.

The lightning sped through his body, linking his mind and soul. Sweat poured from his body until he could no longer contain the inevitable.

His deafening roar shattered the windows.

Lightening poured from his body, touching, destroying everything within the room, leaving smoldering ashes.

His body, his soul, and his mind shook from the waves of aftermath. It took every bit of his focus to send a tracker spiraling through Earth and space until he found what he sought.

Taking one last look at where, and what, he barely lived for in this world, he headed straight for hell.

*

"I'm here. What the hell is going on that I couldn't live my life in peace?" Dante asked.

Esther and Marion, not in the least surprised at his attitude, waited silently as he paced the length of the room, his black boots echoing in the empty room.

The orbs had vanished when he materialized, dressed in black, snarling like a tiger and his body, lean and powerful, ready to tear whatever had backed him in a corner. The orbs wanted no part of violence and left them to quiet the tiger in their midst.

"Son of a—" he roared.

The room shook.

Esther and Marion checked the sky.

It was clear.

They were safe for now.

"Safe?" he laughed, humorously, having heard their unspoken thoughts. "I may not have grown up in that world—" He resumed pacing, looking at his aunts each time he passed. "Do you have any idea what you are dealing with?" He didn't give them a chance to answer, having too much depending on him. "Let me tell you. Apparently, my power has a link that never loses touch with that hell." He stopped in front of them, searching their minds. They weren't expecting him to probe or know the strength of his power from the years of being held prisoner. "You did know. Son of a bitch."

He vanished from the room.

Esther saw the worry on Marion's face. "Don't fret. He's taking care of what needs to be done. No matter what, Dante understands the duties connected with his heritage."

Marion knew that, but would he feel the same after all was said and done?

Chapter Two

Cat Stevens, short for Catherine after her maternal grandmother, had the distinct feeling she was being followed. She wedged into the flowing sidewalk traffic, wearing the same clothing as the locals: jeans, tennis shoes, and a casual shirt, suitable for a warm, fall day. Carrying a small shoulder bag with a few bare necessities in case of an emergency, she held it close to her side, taking in the smallest detail. Past experience taught her to be on the lookout for the expected and unexpected, having hit several dead ends.

Deadly dead ends.

Just when she thought she had found a safe place to hide, people died and accidents happened, forcing her to disappear in the middle of the night. The nightmares began after her grandmother died and Cat had entered *that* house with the devil himself.

In the beginning, David had been a sweet-talking charmer. It hadn't taken long to fall in love with him. In a matter of three months, he had proposed, helped bury her grandmother, and swept her away to his home where he lived with his mother and siblings. A house that is completely evil and mirrored the darkness following her.

Her grandmother, Catherine, had raised her from birth. Cat never knew what happened to her parents, paternal grandparents, or her maternal grandfather. Her grandmother had eloquently avoided all of Cat's questions, saying her curiosity would be her downfall. The day Cat introduced David to her grandmother, Catherine never said an ill word about David or expressed her concerns of Cat and David falling in love so quickly.

That's when Cat knew her grandmother had disapproved.

If her grandmother liked and trusted someone, she made no bones of speaking her mind. Her grandmother always warned Cat to tread lightly when meeting new people and never reveal her hand too quickly.

If that wasn't a large enough red flag to Cat, the moment her grandmother clutched her chest, crumpling to the floor after David's hand touched her shoulder, should've been. Too distraught, Cat had ignored that flag. David had taken care of all the arrangements, seeing to her grandmother's comfort in an exclusive rehabilitation center for patients diagnosed with stroke. He never left Cat's side or her grandmother's, always genuine in his concern for their well-being.

On her grandmother's last night, a nurse came in, informing Cat the doctor wished to speak with her privately. Cat followed her and when she came back, she found David and several staff surrounding her grandmother with the cart, attempting to revive her. Cat had stared in disbelief as a doctor ordered the nurse to wheel the cart away. The doctor shook his head, touching Cat's shoulder as he walked out of the room. David handled the funeral arrangements, settled her grandmother's estate, and whisked her away to his home before she could come out of her fog.

Or acknowledge the reality of those red flags.

It didn't take long for the evil to plague her with horror and death or to find out that David was no longer the David she had fallen in love with.

Luckily, she had the foresight to run away before saying, "I do." It had taken some planning to get away from watchful eyes, but she had done it.

David's rage at her escape could not be hidden, spreading like wildfire through the grapevine. She had run to the family cabin in the mountains, the only thing left of her family.

For some odd reason, her intuition had forewarned not to mention the cabin to David after her grandmother died.

Now she knew why.

It offered the only place left to hide after many months on the run.

But time was running out.

For the past two months, she had stayed in the well-stocked cabin until the meat mysteriously spoiled in the freezer and the garden shriveled up, contaminated from an unknown source, forcing her to seek the local town grocery store.

The air suddenly chilled her to the bone, making her wish she had brought a sweatshirt with her into town. Devil's Falls, located near Hocking Hills, Ohio, was equally picturesque, bringing tourists from all over for the two counties' festivals taking place this weekend. She stopped in front of a shop and unclipped her hair, letting the thickness fall to the middle of her back to help ward off the chill. Placing the clip in her bag, she caught a man staring at her and pretended to search her bag for lip gloss and applied it, using the glass as a mirror.

The guy was tall, clean cut, dressed in slacks and a polo shirt. His smile did not warm the cold eyes staring blatantly or the glacial features mirrored in the glass. He kept his arms close to his body, appearing relaxed with the exception of his hands fidgeting in the pocket of his pants as if they were holding back the emotions wrapped inside of him. Then one hand stilled and curled into a fist, the outline of his knuckles jutting out from the material.

She ran a finger above her lip, wiping away the imaginary excess gloss.

His eyes darkened along with his focus to read her intent. He frowned and seemed to focus harder, pulled back quickly and swore. His frustration actually softened his face. He tensed, removed his fist from the pocket, the tips of something long and narrow peeked out.

She nodded, eyeing his intent, warning she would counter any move he made. And she could. At her grandmother's insistence, she had learned to protect herself. Placing her lip gloss back in her bag, she walked away hoping like hell that hell would not follow or that she could, at least, live one more day. Sensing he had picked up the pace, she glanced in the glass as she passed.

The man was cold and lifeless, his expression unhidden, uncaring who saw him for what he was—an assassin.

She weaved in and out of the throng of tourists.

It didn't detour him from closing the distance.

A large crowd spilled out of the three sets of double doors at the local theater, buying her time.

She had no choice and pushed through the crowd from a long time of practice of avoiding encounters by others who had tried similar attempts.

He tried to go around the people and found it difficult. After several attempts, he began shoving at the crowd. Opening his palm, he revealed a knife. He flipped his wrist out and a long, jagged blade, aimed towards the pavement, made a statement loud and clear. It meant to play with her and death.

The man wanted his prey no matter the cost.

A young girl pointed at the knife and screamed.

Cat took off at a dead run and turned the corner.

The man waited behind the crowd, his body language and expression warning that he was a patient man and this delay was only temporary.

She ran into a store and located the back entrance, escaping into the alleys, dodging in and out of connecting alley ways.

Shadows followed.

He knew where she was every step of the way.

But how?

The shadows never disappeared. Instead they warned he was closing in.

She turned to the open streets, hoping for another delay.

Frantic at the narrowing time, she searched for possible barriers, finding none except a fire escape attached to a hotel and more alleys.

Quickly making a decision, she hooked the ladder with her bag and jumped on as it slid downward within reach. She climbed up and threw her legs over the top railing. A man, a towel wrapped around his waist, his muscular body wet and tense, blocked her escape. Water dripped from his long hair onto her shirt as he moved her to the side, yanking up the ladder. Judging by the rigid jaw line, he wasn't happy to be interrupted.

Not sure if he was friend or foe, she backed away.

His eyes matched his expression as he blocked her escape, holding out his hand for her bag, silently forbidding her to argue.

She didn't want to trust him.

Looking towards the street, she sensed that time was no longer on her side. She had learned long ago to follow her grandmother's intuition and hone her own.

It said to trust no one.

But what choice did she have?

Exhaust her escape routes and die a slow death within hours or trust this man long enough to build her safety nets?

She closed her eyes, hating death following her and the decisions it made her make. Hating to go against what her grandmother had taught her. She could feel his hands tense and opened her eyes, meeting unspoken heat and danger. Yet, those same eyes offered safety. She bit her lip, knowing there was a hidden clause in that safety net.

A metal scraping over brick echoed.

Darkness seeped into her soul.

Evil permeated the air, the blade warning what she had dreamed would all come to fruition in the most heinous ending.

There was no time for analyzing or learning more about his reasons for the safety he offered. She was going to regret this. She just knew it. But if one asked for an extra day of living, who was she to mock this opportunity? Throwing caution to the wind, she quickly handed him her bag and he threw it through the window. He gathered her close, shielding her from the darkness, and wrapped his hand in her thick, auburn hair. Caught between him and the wall, her intuition screamed for her to run as her body tightened, anticipating his touch.

"You have no choice but to trust me." She heard him speak as she stared at those lips, praying they were not deadly. "Or face whatever demon placed the terror in your eyes."

Her lips parted to tell him she didn't trust.

Her intuition warned not to disagree with a man who spoke true words.

Instead, she pulled his lips down to her. He went past the chaste kiss to a full-blown takeover, driving her senses beyond common sense and her body dripping with a growing need she had long forgotten. Her fingers gripped the towel as the whispered words reached her ear, promising he would make her fly high beneath him.

She couldn't think straight.

Couldn't think past her fingers dropping the towel from his body.

She attempted to push him away, knowing she could not afford any distractions. His hands stopped her and placed her own against his chest as he pressed his body into hers. He kissed her neck tenderly, taking her mind in another direction, as his hands held her tighter against him. She whimpered, unable to control the sound escaping her lips or the way her body begged for a release of what he started.

Or had she?

He backed away, breathing hard, fighting for control of his own emotions. She understood why he had backed away. They barely knew each other, yet, there was this sense of connection she couldn't explain. She needed to feel again after all the horror she had witnessed.

He was providing a temporary safe haven in his arms, and she longed to take what he offered.

To lean on someone. To build her strength for what was to come.

She fought to slow her breathing.

"I need to get you inside." He lifted her into his arms, uncaring she could see how she affected him.

She didn't know why, but she let him. Once inside, she would slip through the lobby and disappear.

"Is the person male, pointed nose, blond hair, marine cut?" he asked without fanfare. She nodded, trying to see if the man was below. "He's at the corner of the building, talking on the phone." He gently slipped her through the window and followed, not bothering to grab the towel as it loosened.

The king-size bed gave her mind too many fantasies after the way he had kissed her. She avoided looking at it. The fireplace provided the lighting. Extra logs were stacked nearby. A duffle bag lay unzipped on the dresser. Steam still came from an adjoining room, reminding her that she had interrupted his shower.

"Where does that door lead to?" she asked, watching him head into the bathroom.

"Nowhere."

She was too tired, wishing she could build her energy before disappearing tonight, to push the boundaries of his harsh tone, the unspoken words that said she was not leaving this room.

Chapter Three

Jack keyed in the phone numbers with distaste and waited. He hated Earth's technology. It was outdated and time consuming, but Council wanted it this way, stating it attracted too much attention to ignore it and consequently alerted mutineers that Council was vulnerable if they had to chase a mere girl whose powers were unknown.

Lycon especially was interested in this girl, convincing the rest of the Council members to tag along. Lycon had more than seniority in his power as head chief of Council. He had a vested interest. A personal one. One only Lycon knew, but it was enough to commission Jack's soul from the dead to use his evil and persistence to kill his prey.

Not to mention, Jack had a reputation of never screwing up a contract.

Fingering the tip of the jagged blade, Jack was bound by professional reputation to finish a job before it finished him. Lycon never ceased to remind him that he was on borrowed time each time the Council contracted him. Jack had been a hard negotiator on each contract but failed each time.

Lycon held him by the balls.

To be more precise—his soul.

Jack learned once one settled in with a nest of venomous snakes, one never left on his own.

"Jack, you realize what will happen if you don't succeed?" a voice warned.

Jack twirled the blade in his hand, knowing all too well. "Back down, Lycon. I know my job better than anyone. I created job carving before it ever existed," he answered with arrogance.

Jack may not have the upper hand in contracts—yet—but he held enough power to prevent Lycon from doing any damage. No one had pulled off taking out the original Council members except him, and *that* gave him a high ranking position in his world. He had his own following, and those followers had made Lycon aware they would never take over his contracts with Lycon or his Council members.

"Jack. Jack, my boy…"

Lycon's dismissive tone enraged Jack, pushing the point of his blade into the tip of his finger.

A single drop of blood followed the blade downward.

Jack imagined Lycon's jugular under it. "I am older than you, Lycon." He refused to bow down to anyone and no one could read his mind, which ticked off Lycon.

And scared Lycon into sweating each time it was a stalemate.

"Keep your record spotless," Lycon warned. "I want that girl no matter what it takes. Make it happen."

Jack wasn't in the mood for this drama.

He knew what needed to be done. Lycon just needed patience.

Maybe it was in his best interest to focus on the girl's importance and how it was related to Lycon before he finalized the contract.

Chapter Four

Dante grabbed the towel from the warming bar and dried off. His reflection mocked him in the mirror, warning, as if he hadn't learned enough from the past.

Avoid attachments.

He couldn't afford any complications. His immediate attraction to her, wondering if she wore matching black garments below her black t-shirt and jeans, was a complication he would not take on.

For his sake. And hers.

There was no time for play. He probed her mind and found it blocked. Maybe she had tapped into her potential power and erected a barrier. Projecting his sight into the adjoining room, he saw her sticking her head out the window, checking for whatever terror forced her to climb onto his balcony, and closing the window afterward. She was careful not to touch anything or get too close to his personal belongings.

"Where does that door lead to?" she asked a second time.

"Nowhere." It didn't. Not really. Death leads to nowhere, and if he let her through that door, he will have given hell a new toy. Putting the safeguards in place would have to wait. He did not want to alert her to his powers until he was ready.

A loud crash from the other side of the bathroom wall interrupted his projection. His sight took him to the sound and found two lovers, wrapped in each other's arms, who had bumped into a plant stand.

"If you want something to drink, help yourself to the—" He stopped.

Something wasn't right.

Securing the towel around his hips, he walked into the room, expecting to see the door wide open and an empty room.

The door was closed and she was curled up in the chair closest to the door.

With this girl asleep, she wouldn't be answering his questions. He had tried several times to probe her mind and hit dead ends each time.

For now, she was safe.

He just wasn't sure if he would be.

While she slept, he put on jeans and checked the windows, doors, electrical outlets, vents, anything with an opening. He had learned the hard way to safeguard all entrances and exits. For now, he would allow her to sleep.

*

Dante was aware of the energy shift in the room before he awakened. His mind forewarned him to tread carefully. His powers protected him at all costs, connecting with no one—friend or foe.

Until now.

Something about the girl stirred long-forgotten protective urges.

His mind caught the shadows lurking on the dimly lit balcony. The moon cast enough light to see that the chair was empty and she was nowhere around.

He rolled off the bed, crouching low to the ground.

Only someone from his world, with ancient powers, could penetrate the protection he had secured for the night.

Sending his mind to all areas, he found his barriers untouched. No one entered or exited this room.

But where had she gone? She couldn't have slipped through. Only someone with powers matching his own could pull this off.

Unlocking the barriers, he pushed his sight into every crevice, starting with the bathroom, searching for whomever, or whatever, had taken her.

A shadow crossed in the moonlit room.

It was still in the room.

He reached into the air and grabbed the shadow maker and slammed it against the wall by the throat and held it to the ceiling.

Advancing towards the muffled fury, death by his hand was imminent.

Power, nearly equally his own, radiated from the shadow.

Strange the power did not reach out and try to destroy him. As he closed in, he could feel the fury and the untapped power, begging to be released.

He also scented something else.

Slowly lowering the shadow into the moonlight, he smiled, now recognizing the scent and the shadow maker. There was only one way to find answers and that was to find a way to connect. He loosened his hold on the shadow maker. This time, he knew he couldn't back away from his duty.

"Where do you think you were going?" he asked.

He dodged the furious kicks aimed for his face, advanced closer and secured the legs and arms to the wall effortlessly with his mind.

The answer to his question radiated from the violet eyes.

Her eyes.

Placing his hands on the wall, he leaned in and whispered as he lowered her, "Let me in."

"Back off. You think I'd let just anyone in? There's nothing between us."

He didn't dare laugh. "Would you like to see?"

His fingers skimmed in the air, having the ability to feel without actually touching physically. He skimmed her neckline and traced between her breasts, before resting his hand above her soul.

"Hell will freeze over, lover boy," she spit out, hating the slight hitch of her breath calling her a liar.

Just as he knew better than to laugh at having proven her wrong, she should've known better than to throw out a challenge.

He moved his hand over her heart. To feel what he was feeling. She tried to shake off his hold, to not acknowledge him, but the power he wielded was much stronger and forced her to look at him. Her blood surged, speeding up her heart, quickening the beat. He saw the slight rise and fall as she tried to fight the adrenaline of need. To not give into the emotion of feeling again.

He moved his hand near her abdomen and smiled as her body tightened and she bit her lip, but not before he heard her response. He sought entrance to her mind, her body. To her soul. She blocked him. He focused harder. His sight began to shake.

It was then he noticed she was shaking.

The power from within her, one he had not recognized until now, was growing stronger the longer he touched her, the more he pushed her to feel, to want.

"I will let you down if you tell me your name. You are safe here." At least from the shadows outside.

"Oh, please. You expect me to believe that when you are hard as hell and holding me up here like a puppet. I don't know what the hell you are, but I want no part of it," she said, refusing to open her eyes as if it were taking everything she had in holding him away.

He couldn't read her mind, but could feel her insides bursting from the fury of her power, pushing her body to the limits.

"I'm not going to say it again." He refused, finding it a waste of their time when there were shadows outside and lives at stake.

He wanted to touch.

Wanted an excuse.

"Don't touch," she ordered, her eyes flying open.

He dropped his hand to his side. "Hmmm … How interesting … a cat with violet eyes." Even more interesting how her senses detected his movement.

He studied her, wanting to touch her again, to feel her smooth skin, the power screaming to be released in more ways than one.

There was another way to touch her, but there would be too many questions if he did it here.

Chapter Five

"Do you want to see a cat or talk to Cat?"

"Maybe I would like to provoke the cat within Cat," Dante provoked, touching the inside of her leg.

Knowing it was futile to free herself or to prevent him from baiting her, she forced her true reaction of his touch to stay hidden. "You can try, but this kitty has claws."

"I'm sure you have very sharp ones."

Damned if she could fight the power holding her much longer, but she still had her attitude.

She had failed to follow her own rules, and it almost cost her life. While she was pinned to this wall, she had to take every moment and use it to her advantage. There was more to meeting this guy than a mere coincidence. He may not have been expecting her, but he knew of her and that was enough to keep her on guard.

His body was in true warrior form, in strength and power. Lethal and persuasive with one touch. Looking into those dark blue eyes almost made her forget to close off. If there was one thing she had learned when she had lived in that house with David, it was how to block images or emotions of any kind. If she could block the horrific images and their intruding probes from her mind, then she could handle this man.

These days she had become a realist versus a glass-half-full kinda girl.

One look into those eyes of his told her she was in deep trouble.

In ways she was not prepared to handle.

When he released her, and he would in his own sweet time, she would run like hell.

She had to push the attraction away, focus on her next move and surroundings.

"You asked for a name and I gave it. Let me down." Others had backed off instantly by the look she had given him, but it only made him smile.

"Bossy, too."

"Bite me," she said, lifting her chin in defiance.

Dante laughed. "Little cat, do not tempt me."

Most people didn't take that literally, but the intent in his eyes said he was about to.

"You don't understand," she whispered as his thumb caressed her mouth, her teasing her senses. Desperate to stop the rising emotions, every effort to speak was a struggle. "Stop—"

He stopped, serious as the hell following her. "You don't understand. You're not leaving my sight."

Her blood surged. She could feel it rising and struggled to prevent it. "Damnit—whatever the hell your name is—release me!"

"It's Dante." His thumb returned and stroked her lower lip, staring thoughtfully before releasing her.

She dropped on all fours.

He walked away, uncaring that she ready to pounce. "Sheath the claws and play nice."

Cat hissed as she stood up.

She wasn't anyone's play toy—even if she was attracted to him.

"Look, I appreciate the use of your room. I'm fine and it's time I headed home. It's been hours since I've been followed," she changed tactics.

He went into the bathroom, stopped in front of the vents, and moved to the window. "You are safer in here than out there. I am taking you to a safer place."

"What are you looking for?" she asked, blocking the bathroom entry.

He started to squeeze past, apparently deciding against it, for she found her body rising once more and transported, this time gently, out of the way.

"Checking the protection seals I had put in place."

"I don't know you from Adam, and you could be as dangerous as that guy wielding a knife."

"Knife?" He did a double take, stopping in his tracks. "Describe it."

"I sensed someone following me. The window was a great front so I could check out my surroundings casually. He knew I'd spotted him and didn't bother to blend in with the crowd. As I passed a theater, a large group came pouring out just as he pulled his hands out of his pocket and flipped out a knife. The length of the jagged blade was about six inches long, narrowing to needle point tip. It was all black. I wouldn't have noticed what it looked like if a young girl hadn't screamed and pointed at what the guy was holding. For whatever reason, no one tried to apprehend him. He stayed on my trail, never losing sight of me, even when he could no longer physically see me."

Dante's facial expression was set in stone, no longer questioning.

"You know who he is," she said.

"Enough to know you're definitely not leaving my sight. I didn't recognize the man on the corner, but if he is the owner of that knife, then someone who wants you dead or alive—I'm not sure which at this moment—has decided to pull out the heavy weights."

"I'm not buying it. Freaky things happen to people all the time. I just happened to be in the wrong place at the wrong time."

"You're kidding me, right?" he lounged against the dresser, his eyes mocking her.

"Can you think of something better?"

"Yes. The truth. Truth you aren't ready to hear tonight."

She had not witnessed any murders. No mafia connections, unless you count a very wealthy man, like David, intent on possessing and drawing her into an evil family. Not that she had seen the evil firsthand, just the screams she heard during the night.

The wicked laughter, a hair above a whisper, seeping from ceilings. Some nights she swore blood had dripped down the walls in her bedroom.

Other than David wanting what he couldn't have, she thought ironically, she had no clue as to why anyone would go to such lengths to hunt her down.

Too much was happening in the last few months for her to be able to think.

She needed out of here, on her own and free without jeopardizing anyone's safety. She didn't need her body lusting after something she couldn't have.

And right now, she wanted him.

"It doesn't matter. I'm not involving you in my drama. I don't even want to be within ten feet of it."

"What you or I want is not relevant at this moment. It has been taken out of our hands. There's nothing we can do but meet whatever is coming for you head on."

She wasn't buying that nothing could be done about this situation. The double-edged meaning behind the words and the fire in his eyes were loud and clear. He wanted her in a bad way, yet, refused to surrender to it every time he checked her out. It was as if he wanted to pin her to the wall and get her out of his system for this attraction taking away his lack of control over his own mind and body.

"Sure there is. You go your way and I go mine." She gave him a smile that clearly told him she knew what was bothering him.

She didn't understand why she had done it, but she cocked her head, daring Dante.

He was in front of her in seconds, dragging her back against the wall, pinning her with his hands, stealing that dare from her lips. Fire consumed her, pushing her over the edge as she ran her hands over his bare skin, feeling the flex of his biceps. Her fingertips followed his torso and dipped between the jeans. He tensed, slightly moving from her touch. She dipped lower, skimming her fingertips and nearly sighed with pleasure. Delving deeper to show him just how high she could push him. She almost succeeded before he backed up and wrapped his hand around her wrist.

He pulled her hand out and held it behind her back. She gave him a cocky smile, telling him she wasn't finished by a long shot and to accept what he dished out. The dark, smoldering heat in his eyes warned her not to go for it or he would finish it the way he wanted.

As she reached with her other hand to unbutton his jeans, she wondered if her grandmother had called her Cat because of her unanswered curiosity, this need to push things to the limit, to see how many lives she could go through.

And now her curiosity for this man and what kind of lover she could handle—having never gotten past those few times with David, who, she later learned, was fighting to keep the evil at bay—was rising hard and furious. The past year she had learned to read people fast in order to survive.

Dante was different.

He had a hardened edge about him and looked as if he kept everyone at a distance, never losing control; yet, deep down she knew he wasn't evil.

Would he be a dark or easy lover?

His hand tightened over hers, warning he was nearing his limit—or rather she was—if she pushed any further.

She pushed the button through with her thumb, watching his eyes darken as she ignored the warning.

He had her other hand joined behind her back in no time flat as he backed her to the wall, his expression guttural and dark at being pushed past that limit. "You had to do it, didn't you? Well, let's see what my cat has decided to play with," he said, his lips searing her neck. "Never play with a tomcat, Cat. Tomcats play for keeps."

Her female intuition warned her she had gone too far. The beat of her libido said she hadn't pushed far enough for him to lose total control, while her blood surged like lava. Hot. Dangerous. Liquid heat begging to be released.

By him.

Trembling made it difficult to hold onto the waistband of his jeans. Her fingertips slid free, unable to hold on any longer and latched onto his zipper, sliding it down. The rasp of the teeth and his quick intake of breath signaled a new level of playing was about to begin.

Chapter Six

Dante fought the rising emotions of wanting and needing to be inside her, to take her higher than he had ever taken anyone. Since the moment she had climbed up the ladder, make-up free, her hair tussled as if she'd just walked away from an all-nighter of passion and was still ready to go with those violet eyes screaming for release, he had wanted her.

She had hesitated scant seconds before caving to his touch.

The little cat had dared to try to escape, dared to be free with her responses. Dared to push his control buttons. Dared to touch him in ways he had never allowed, gaining access without his permission.

And now he had to play this out.

He would never allow her full reign. It didn't matter he had responded to her dares and attempts to control the situation—what he should be doing was fulfilling his obligations as quickly as possible.

Yet, she enticed him in so many ways from his main focus.

Her delectable little mouth whispered soft cries of pleasure.

The arch of her body granted him permission.

The slight tilt of her head accepted the heat.

His body raged a war of its own against him, making him forget past lessons to never let a woman near him.

And this woman made his mind and body forget what it had learned.

He slid his hand under her shirt, the smooth, silky skin heating his flesh. Her nipples hard under the lacy material barely covering it. Slipping a finger under the lace, he brushed over it with his forefinger, wanting to elicit more of those cries.

There was no going back the moment he had accepted the power he had forsaken, no matter how much he hoped to vanish once it was over. He would taste her body in every way and hope like hell there was no hell lurking around the corner to interrupt what was his for the taking or steal her before he had a chance to fulfill his duty.

He palmed her other breast, brushing his thumb across her nipple. Taking control was the best way at this time. He kissed her, slipping his tongue inside, daring to meet those soft cries before they escaped her beautiful mouth.

He was not disappointed.

A small tremor shook her body.

An afterglow of foreplay.

Maybe if one of them, or both, came they could focus on getting out of this situation alive instead of burning up from this rising heat between them. The more he tasted the cries flowing from her lips, the more her body trembled with force, the intensity suggesting the hidden power beneath the surface. His gut reaction demanded he push the power past no return.

But would she be able to handle it?

No one knew what powers Jack the Ripper was granted in his contract to bring her back.

Or why this particular little cat was so important when there were so many powers to manipulate, to destroy.

The tremors did not slow when he backed off, continuing to hit again and again, throwing her into complete shock.

He swept her into his arms as her knees buckled and carried her to the bed. Laying her down gently, he located the flow of energy immediately with his sight and found her dormant powers seeping into her body, pushing at Cat's control. Deciding to see where the leakage originated, he whispered he would enter her body with his sight, hoping she would hear him. She gave a small nod of understanding. Short, quick breaths made it difficult for her lungs to breathe properly, judging by the rise and fall of her chest.

He needed to see how much his touch had initiated her energy's response. He touched her earlobe with his tongue. The energy flow did not increase. She nodded as if understanding. He kissed her thoroughly, unable to stop his male pride as she responded. He tasted the sweet energy her tongue offered as it met his. His body absorbed all that it offered him. The tremors subsided from her body and he pulled away. When the shock did not wear off, he probed her mind, hoping there were no barriers.

It was locked down tight.

What would happen if he used her energy from within to destroy it?

He barely caught the hand flying his way. That's what happened when he forgot about keeping a woman at a distance. "My, my, we are touchy about destroying your mind barrier but not your virginity?" He laughed at her outrage.

"Let me up." She struggled to push him off. "What makes you think I'm a virgin?"

He released her hand and moved away before she had time to aim again. "I forgot my catnip, so let's take a breather," he said, struggling not to laugh at the spitting fury at his comment or her muttered words, "Catnip my ass."

She swung her legs to the side as she sat up, wincing as dizziness hit.

He stepped forward, ready to catch her.

"What the hell happened?"

He tried keeping a straight face and failed, liking the effect he had on her despite the interference she had on his focus. She was cute, sexy, and a spitfire. "You don't remember going into shock right after you came? So much for my technique," he winced.

She rolled her eyes, not buying the soulful expression, and fell backwards.

He was by her side instantly, surprised at the worry eating away inside him.

She waved him away, her eyes still closed, trying to catch her breath, but he didn't budge. "I'm fine. Your manly pride remains intact. No one has ever made me fly like that." She shook off a tremor threatening to rush in and tried to sit up, failing.

As much as he'd like to take credit for making her spin out of control, whatever held her powers dormant and kept her knowledge in the dark, contributed to those tremors.

He had to find out how dangerous it would be, for her sake, if the dam broke loose.

Not wanting to think of anyone else triggering those same emotions or energy surges, he watched her fight to regain control.

"Talk to me. And not what you'd like to do to me," she smiled into the words. "About why you had this expression as if you knew me. Granted, there was a surprised look, too, but I felt like the fly climbing into the spider's home."

Dante leaned in the shadows, sensing she was deciding how much she should divulge. He didn't have long to wait.

"Like I said … I think I was in the wrong places at the wrong times."

"If there's more than one, you still think it was being in the wrong place?" he asked, angry at the danger she placed herself in and not protecting herself better. "How many times?"

"A couple."

"Cat," he demanded.

She sighed. "Does it really matter?"

The shadows hid his expression. "If you want to live."

Nothing like backing her into a corner to make her come out dragging her heels was shouting from the way her body tensed. "Oh, I will live." She moved towards the door.

He dropped his arms and uncrossed his boot, moving between her and the door.

"So help me, Cat, you are the most stubborn—"

She smiled. "Seven."

She had played him, but it would be the last time. Watching through narrowed eyes, he settled back. "Lives or wrong places?"

"Lives?" She laughed at the intensity of his expression. "If I didn't know any better, I'd say you knew my grandmother." She held up hand, still laughing. "Places."

"For how long?"

The laughter died. "A year ago. I thought it was just a fluke happening. I had barely crossed the street on my way to apply for a job when someone pulled me from being road kill. The black van careened into several parked cars."

"Trying to miss an animal or another car and didn't see you?"

"No. The road was clear with the exception of the man who pulled me to safety. When he introduced himself as Jeremiah and opened the door to check on the driver, we found the van empty. The windows were darkened," she answered, seeing the unspoken question. "After Jeremiah left, I went inside to follow up on my interview appointment. The place was empty. I thought I had the wrong address and tried calling the owner. The number had been disconnected."

"After that first accident, I drove into a few towns and finally lucked out as someone was getting fired for fudging the books. For a week, everything seemed quiet. It was a cozy little one horse town. Then weird things started happening. Every time I touched someone, they ended up dying."

Chapter Seven

If Cat thought she didn't have his full attention before, she had it now.

"They dropped like flies—that kind of dying?" Dante asked.

"Not at first. You're not going to believe this. I had become friends with a few co-workers and we hugged after doing a girls' night out at a restaurant. They were both killed instantly by a hit-and-run driver as they crossed the street. A fluke. Or so I thought.

"The next day, I helped an elderly woman cross the street and she died at my feet. The paramedics said it was probably a heart attack. When the paramedic put his hand on my shoulder to comfort me—I guess I looked awful—he was shot in front of us." Oh hell, those had been hard reliving, but the next was devastating. She closed her eyes, willing the tears back.

"It got around about me and the wake of deaths to the point people were crossing the other side of the street. I quit my job, knowing the owner was a single mom and her kid had no other family. I couldn't take the chance. I thought if I left in the middle of the night, whatever, whoever was following me, creating devastation, would leave them alone. I had driven twelve hours and stopped at a larger city, hoping I would be less visible. I grabbed the help wanted ads from the counter, waiting for a table. A young mother was trying to juggle her infant and find her car keys. When she asked if I could hold him for a second, without even thinking about it, I accepted the baby in my arms..."

"That's okay, Cat. I get the picture. I'm not even sure I can handle what you're about to say, but there's one thing you haven't mentioned."

She opened her eyes, trying to keep the memories and the tears at bay.

"What have the police said about the string of incidents?" he asked, then drew his own conclusion when she rolled her eyes in disbelief. "Let me guess. They thought you were the culprit."

She grinned. "Worse. They considered me a nut job." She didn't make him wait. "When they investigated, the bodies had disappeared. No witnesses. No bodies. They literally had disappeared. From the morgue. From the town."

"Didn't you say the townspeople avoided you like the plague?"

"Yes, even after the police questioned them."

"You said there were seven deaths. What about the other two?"

"After the baby, I couldn't take any chances. I felt as if I had the plague. I traveled around, using some money I had saved back, keeping cost to a minimum by parking in secluded wooded areas." She ignored the look she received. "When no one else appeared to drop from death, I began to relax. Of course, that was a big mistake. I had decided to call the last place home for a few months. I kept to myself. Didn't touch anyone and worked on blocking my heart, mind, and spirit from negativity."

"In other words, you shut yourself off from the world to survive."

Cat never thought anyone would get how she was feeling—until Dante brought it to the surface. He had understood what she had done and why. "I had to. Then ... I ... I let someone through my defenses—" She tried to block out the humanity, those seeking for a human touch, a heart.

"They paid dearly. Didn't they?" he asked softly, approaching.

She nodded, too choked up to speak, allowing him to draw her into his embrace. The tears fell. She had never given into this emotion, knowing it would put her at a disadvantage. Dante's words had hit too close to home, speaking volumes of understanding, a hidden meaning of somehow having similar experiences.

It had been a very long time since she had allowed anyone but David to hold her—in fact, not since her grandmother had died. Cat missed her terribly. There had been a strength about this woman who raised her. She hadn't realized it until tonight, but her grandmother had kept everyone at bay. Except Cat. There wasn't a day when Cat never went without hugs. Cat had heard her grandmother's friends whispering when they thought she had left the room, stating anytime they opened their hearts to love, it left room for mistakes when so many children, their heritage, their world was in danger of being extinct.

Undoubtedly, the love her grandmother had shown brought death to her door. By not sharing Cat's heritage, Cat had brought the danger home.

David.

There were too many deaths, too many supernatural incidents and not enough answers.

If he needed answers from her, she might as well get help finding answers to her own questions.

Wrapped in his arms, she didn't dare enjoy the soothing touch of his hand on her back too much or she would lose sight of the situation. Her grandmother's love for Cat, allowed the heart to cloud the mind—and Cat couldn't afford to let this happen with her, but his scent reminded her of outdoors and mystery, pushed past her reserves, drawing the need to touch him. To quench the need to feel human once again.

And if she were truly honest with herself, she wanted to feel her heart beat for passion and not terror.

His bare chest, the defined body, the safety in his arms, the strength beneath her fingertips only made her want to touch every bit of his body.

She forced herself to not cave into her curiosity and desires.

His hand slipped under her shirt, the direction and method changed with purpose.

"Let me in," he whispered.

She shook her head.

The rhythm of his fingers crooned.

Surprise, shock, and exhilaration hit her at once.

He was summoning her energy flow, going against her wishes. She had to get out of here before she lost total control. If she gave into her desires, would she be safe?

Dante's first wave of action was to get the answers he needed, hell-bent on completing his own mission. She was just as taken back by their chemistry explosion as he was, but they needed to separate or they would find life a dead end for both of them.

Suddenly his fingers stopped, and he tensed as if listening for something.

"What's wrong?" she asked, pulling out of his embrace.

"They're evacuating the building. There's a bomb threat. I might be able to help, but you will need to stay in this room. I can't watch you and deactivate the bomb."

Like she was going to do as he asked. "How do you know it's not a false alarm?"

"I found where it's located, but I can't deactivate it from here." He grabbed a black t-shirt from his bag and put it on.

"Why do you need to deactivate it?" She really wanted to ask how he knew, but it wasn't the time. Surprised at the rising worry for his safety, she found herself blocking him from the door—as if that would stop a man like Dante.

He picked her up by the shoulders and moved her aside. "You and I have too much in common, besides this explosive chemistry that we need to explore further. Between my facts and yours, we can put it all together. And maybe," he said, sliding the clip into his gun, "We might just get out of here alive." He stared, his expression wicked and promising. "I don't have time to set up the safeguards, so if you run, you're endangering both of us. Until we solve all of your pieces, it will be harder to get to you in time if the killer reaches you first."

Cat knew she was going to run.

She had to.

Just as he knew she would run.

He looked at her. "Cat?" She nodded her understanding. "Good."

Dante unlocked the final safeguard and gave her a silent warning to stay put.

She didn't have anything other than her bag, so she granted herself one last look. Blowing out a small sigh of appreciation as he raced down the hall, fighting against the clock, she turned to get her bag and ran smack into the assassin.

"Going somewhere?" Jack asked.

She didn't see his knife, but the smell of death permeated the room and into her pores. It had the same nasty side effect of making her nauseous as the house she had escaped.

"You planted the bomb."

"Good observation. Have others?"

"I don't know what or who you and Dante are, but, I'm betting that bomb is something only Dante can get near."

The satisfaction of his intent was very clear. "Your grandmother never mentioned me?" he changed the subject.

Wary, she shook her head, deciding it was best to acknowledge this to gain answers.

He tsk-tsk'd. "I'm saddened she gave me no introductions, considering—well, never mind, for now. We'll have enough time for that later. First, I like having order to my deaths. You are not at the top of my list at this second. So be a good girl and vamoose. Shoo!"

The window flew open and her handbag landed at her feet.

When she didn't move, the bag was tossed from the ground to her hand, and he gave her a body a nudge with his powers.

Half-way out the window, knowing she couldn't do anything to help Dante, she still paused. "You could've taken me out any time. Why didn't you use whatever source your body houses?" she asked.

"Intelligent." He stepped into the hallway. "Let's just say, there's something about the thrill of hunting that I miss the most from the old days."

Chapter Eight

Jack didn't give a damn if Lycon had seen him push Cat away. Not in the sense a normal person wouldn't give a damn.

But then, he wasn't a normal person.

He laughed.

When had he ever been normal? He didn't want to think about it, because for a time, before Lycon, a very short time, he had tasted normal. He could almost understand the idea of being screwed when he had been offered the most exquisite, unobtainable game of all.

Hunting the unseen. The not-so-normal.

And what did he gain from it?

Not a damn thing.

Because someone like Lycon never gave up what he owned.

And Jack refused to give up *everything* he owned.

Jack was his own man.

Not the humans of today. Not police or weaponry. Not losing his average prey for Lycon had almost given him the ultimate world.

Souls that never forgot the pain, the horror, the exquisite agony of being hunted.

And, like one of his favorite movies, those souls relived it over and over again.

Jack had the curiosity of a cat, not liking it when someone held his soul as collateral. In order to increase his chances of escaping Lycon, Jack had dug deeper, surprised at the secrets he had uncovered. It seemed Lycon had fathered a child.

Cat.

Lycon had eyes and ears all over the place and someone would snitch if he didn't look as if he were doing Lycon's bidding. In due time, he would take out Dante and Cat, but for now, creating small diversions kept Lycon from getting too close to Jack's plans. The bombs he left behind were invitations to those who knew him so well. This particular one Dante would recognize. Jack didn't rush off to Dante. He had left plenty of time for Dante and Cat to be far away from here to lead him to more answers and time.

There were times Jack liked the old-fashioned way of not transporting from place to place. It may not be the suspense that killed them, but he there was pure pleasure in watching their faces as he walked towards them.

Only Jack knew as he took the last few steps towards the rooftop, Dante would not have terror in his eyes.

The door flew open before Jack's hand touched the handle.

Dante stood by the air vent, his stance and hands flexed for battle.

The wind added its displeasure, pushing everything in its path.

"Hello, old friend," Jack said. "I had heard you had disappeared and thought you were dead. The expression of one assuming still holds up. How did you survive this long?"

"Seclusion keeps one safe. I didn't know it was you until your special bomb found its way here. Our families were from the same side of town. I may not have looked for trouble, but I sure as hell don't back down from it."

"What brought you out of seclusion?" Jack didn't make any sudden movements onto the rooftop. Dante had a hair trigger temper if riled, and Jack didn't like not being the first one to make a move. "It's like old times."

Dante nodded with resolution. "It doesn't have to be."

"It's the same then as it is now." Jack didn't gloat. He never did just before he killed. Never after. It made watching one's back harder than it needed to be.

"You sent your usual invite."

Jack smiled at the tone of words, choosing it as a compliment. "You liked? A compliment from you is rare."

Dante returned the smile, shaking his head. "That one is a genuine compliment. Even I couldn't have done any better. For old times' sake…" He gestured to the air vent for Jack to deactivate the bomb.

Jack couldn't. He had to follow through in some way, even if it wasn't the way Lycon wanted. Jack had his ethics, and he would not deviate compared to Lycon, who had none among fellow killers.

"I can't do it. I let your toy run away. I'm letting you run away."

"So kind of you," Dante mocked. "Aren't you ready to retire?"

Jack held up his hands in momentary surrender as he stepped onto the rooftop, positioning himself. "Do you know retired killers are mocked for being bouncers in other worlds? Holy shit! There's no way I can lower to that level. It's all or nothing. Does she know?"

"Cat? She knows of the evil following her. You. The plague of death and unnatural happenings. That she is housing something powerful she is not ready to unleash or understand."

Jack frowned. "Today is the first day I laid eyes on her." Damned if someone was poaching on his territory. When he found out who it is, he would literally skin them alive. "There is one thing I did find out, which will make locating your play toy much easier, is that she owns a cabin in the hills and headed there now."

Jack swept his hand, shoving Dante off the roof.

Dante hovered in mid-air and slammed Jack against the brick wall. "The bomb."

Jack shoved Dante away, sending him flying, and disappeared, but not before he made a promise. "No one will die. Today."

Chapter Nine

Cat longed for a hot bath and a beer as she ran along the off-beaten path in the dark, which her grandmother made her memorize as a child, but she couldn't afford to take the time to heat the bath water or ice down the beer from her last visit once she reached her destination. Her grandmother told her to visit here as often as it took to keep her heritage alive. Cat never thought she would have to rely on childhood memories to keep her alive. Literally. Too many things were happening all at once in this town to be a coincidence.

Hiding from the plague on her tail. The killer. The man who wanted to summon the surge of energy from her soul whether she wanted it or not.

Hell was probably easier than the life she was leading now.

Within days of her arrival, the foliage had blackened to the point of no return, despite the amount rain the area had received. She hadn't made it to the store for supplies and now she had to run again. It wouldn't be long before Dante or the killer located this place. The cabin was a simple structure of logs, yet a place of tranquility.

Until now.

Now all she saw was devastation and the end of the only thing left keeping the memory of her grandmother alive. She never knew her family. A sense of belonging. Not one single article of clothing or jewelry or a picture existed in her presence.

Cat had tried asking how her parents met, their names, where they were, but her grandmother never revealed a single detail. It was as if it were best to keep it all hidden away.

Cat brushed the branches out of the way as she turned and twisted, realizing the path was taken care of even after all these years. Someone else knew of this path, and that meant it was time to leave. She came to the end but stopped short of bursting in to the backyard, waiting for any sign of the killer, stalker, some type of plague.

The grass, plants, trees, and crops were black from death. The chimney was free of smoke. The cabin serene, peaceful, and empty. She crept along the tree line until she was behind the cabin. Sensing no one around, she opened the door, scooted inside, and bolted the door behind her. Without looking around, her instincts said she was safe for now. The living room brought memories of her grandmother. The scratchy, rose-colored rocking chair with matching ottoman. The picture box on the wall was very old, her grandmother had once told her. The wooden bench sat against the wall, matching the kitchen table.

She sat on the rug, tired, wanting this to horror to end but without taking her life. She wished her grandmother was still around to ask questions. Maybe now the woman would be willing to share. Too tired to walk around, Cat wondered what secrets her grandmother wanted her to unearth in the other rooms from the mysterious warnings to keep her heritage close.

The old wood stove, its pipe hooked to the wall, was ice cold. The wood, however, was cured and ready to ignite by one tiny spark upon its bark. The table and benches were made from a fallen oak tree, crude and well-preserved. The kitchen sink resembled those in mud rooms of today. An old butcher's block stood in the center of the room. Pots and pans hung from the iron wrought holder. Her grandmother never replaced the stove and oven, preferring the wood-stoked flames over electricity. The old-fashioned ice box always amazed her, though it was never used. Thinking of ice cold beer quenching the dust from her throat was enough to open it up and look for old time sake.

Four ice cold bottles of beer stood inside.

She closed it and re-opened.

They were still there, yet her senses said she was alone.

The bathroom was as close to modern convenience as her grandmother allowed. A basin with a hand pump spigot, the piping extended to the back of the table and through the wall, sat on a small table. A lit oil lamp hung on the wall, a glass plate protecting the log wall from dangers of fire. Steam rose from the claw tub in the corner.

She walked closer and trailed her fingers in the water with floating rose petals scenting the room.

The water was real. Warm. Inviting.

Before she caved to the cold beer and warm bath, she needed to check the bedroom. It was simple and efficient for sleeping, and it was empty, reminding she was alone in her fight to stay alive. She checked the locks, knowing there wasn't a snowball's chance in hell of blocking the plague bound to sniff her out.

Part of her hoped she wouldn't have to go it alone.

Get real, she laughed at herself. You inherited your grandmother's lack of trust in people and her instinct for survival. Though neither of them anticipated being cornered in all directions. Cat dropped her clothes and was about to step into the tub when she remembered the beer. Not caring she was nude, she walked into the kitchen and grabbed a cold one, twisted off the tab, took the first guzzle of ice down her throat and sighed with pleasure. Setting the beer on the floor next to the tub, she stepped in and sunk into her next pleasure.

If she were being logical, she would care about the waiting ice cold beer and hot bath.

Right now, she didn't want to be logical.

What she wanted was to feel refreshed, human, and relax her mind. She reached for the longneck bottle and took a drink, allowing her mind to be free of barriers.

In a moment, a scene that had not taken place between her and Dante began to play out.

"You are not human. At least not fully human."

Damned if that didn't beat all to hell and back. It was too good to be true. All her pleasures in one place and no time to enjoy them.

"Hello, Dante. I guess I have you to thank for the beer and bath?" She opened her eyes to him lounging in the doorway, one boot hooked over the other one. "Couldn't have shared your shortcut with me?"

"Then I wouldn't have time to provide a few added pleasures before we finish our Q & A. You haven't eaten, and you will need to keep up your strength."

She took another long drink and heard the twist of a cap, surprised when a cold one replaced her already tepid one. "Thank you. Ahhh ... a man who shops *and* cooks. If I had a normal life with lots of girlfriends, they'd say snatch you up and not let go." She saluted her bottle in the air and gave a saucy wink, slightly tipsy from lack of food. "But then, from the deaths, plague, assassin, being lifted and held on a wall by powers unknown, I'd say," she took another long drink, "this is as far away from a normal life as one gets."

"I will give you ten minutes to bathe, and I will be back to collect you before you drown."

She heard the amusement in his voice. Sexy and very male. One who seemed to think he could do whatever he wanted. "What makes you think I need a nursemaid?"

He took the bottle from her hand hanging over the side, not bothering to hide his laughter. "Your eyes are closed and you are losing a damn good beer to the floor. Both of you need saving."

She listened to the footsteps fade away. "I didn't hear the bottle touch the table."

"I didn't go to all that work to let a good bottle of beer go to waste." He was silent for a long moment and then male appreciation of a low whistle followed.

Suddenly, Cat couldn't breathe, barely hearing the bottle hit the floor. Her heart beat faster and faster. She couldn't open her eyes. Couldn't move. Seizures racked her body. Panic racked her mind, and she screamed for Dante to hear her cries for help.

No sound came to her ears.

Her veins raged with blood, energy, and power, rushing at her lungs, cutting off her air supply.

As everything went black, she realized her only hope was for him to go against her wishes and find a way in.

Chapter Ten

Dante wanted to kick someone's ass. His, for taking family duty to heart after so many years of trying to forget the screwed up world he had been born into, and the family for choosing sides.

And now emotions he had never wanted to feel again had resurfaced and he couldn't prevent it.

One woman had brought his hell and his heart back into his life.

Nothing like having them slam you from both sides.

He laughed. Not even an ice cold beer was going to help today. He'd come a long way from those ancient days hiding out in Timbuktu time, limiting the use of his powers to keep him alive from witch hunts and off the radar in Earth's and his world's growing technology. Revisiting a love-hate relationship with an old friend rising from the dead was not anticipated.

Dante had barely survived the death match in his youthful years. He had not expected Council to raise an enemy scorned.

Nor had he expected to get an opportunity to have all his questions answered.

Jack was supposed to have died a death that would have prevented his soul from rising ever again. If he hadn't seen the brand on the bomb, he would never have known Jack's soul had lived. Jack was as surprised as he that moment on the rooftop seeing their existence was a reality.

Even more surprising Jack had let Cat walk away unharmed and provided a link to her whereabouts.

Dante had arrived at the cabin long before Cat, allowing him time to set safeguards on the property's boundaries and give him the chance to care of his cat while he could before hell came fast on their heels.

Hopefully, his cat liked warm baths and would not be hissing after sampling his peace offerings.

And she would be more than willing to hear him out.

He grabbed an iced beer from the fridge, noticing one was missing. He figured there was no time like the present to announce his presence, if she hadn't already guessed he was here.

He followed the splashing sounds and found her soaking in the tub half asleep. Sometimes he'd learned it was better to not disturb sleeping cats, like dogs, and to watch from a distance, but he couldn't. Not anymore than he could walk away from his aunts, the impending destruction of those caught in the middle of the war. He had refused to take sides back then, and to know he had been dragged, implicating him as a traitor to the other side—not that he really gave a damn—but sometimes, life made you take a stand whether you wanted to or not—even if it forced you back into a hell best not revisited.

He switched out her beer for a fresh one. Little did she know, her powers were leaking into her energy level stream, having no place to go as they overflowed from the rising power held at bay, and being absorbed into his bloodstream, granting him limited access to her mind. He heard her wish to feel human without all the drama, and he wanted to tell her she would.

But he couldn't.

He wasn't about to let her live in a fantasy world.

There was no time like the present to start the conversation. "You are not human. At least not fully human."

How the hell was he supposed to give her a history lesson on their world in such short time? He would rather carry her to bed and show her what he'd learned throughout his time. Her spitfire bantering only made him want to push her for more. To capture her lips and tease the words into sighs of pleasure.

Except, Jack was on their heels, and for whatever reason, he was taking his sweet time.

How many times had he and Jack played their hands? Gone toe to toe, power to power and came up stalemate, each and every time? So, why had he felt a surge within the strength of his own powers? Good ol' Jack must be thinking the same thing, considering the look on his face when they had parted.

The water swooshed behind him.

He had hoped the coldness would take the heat down a notch and did what any man, fully human or not, would've done.

He turned.

She was almost asleep, her hand relaxing over the side where she'd left it. The rose petals lapped over her breasts, circulating the surface of the water as her feet lifted slightly out of the water. Allowing herself to drift, her hair had slipped into the water.

He reached forward to push it back over the edge and froze. The bottle slipped from his grasp, crashing to the floor.

The water churned without any aid. A strange glow emerged between the petals.

His cat lay there unaware. Her fingers twitched periodically, and the glow became stronger. The glow seemed familiar to him. Her breathing hitched with each intake. Her hand spasmed. Her body began to shake and she slipped under water.

He rushed over and scooped her out of the tub.

The rush of energy overflow absorbed into his system, hitting him hard and fast. If he struggled to deal with the overflow, he couldn't imagine how her body was handling it. If her powers weren't released soon, she would be in trouble. He carried her into the bedroom and wrapped her in a blanket, using his powers to dry her as she began to convulse.

"Cat, you need to come back to me," he said, rubbing her arms and hands.

She didn't respond.

There were only two ways to bring her back, and he refused to go to the second one—the most extreme and dangerous.

He focused his sight on entering her body.

The energy current within her raged. She didn't seem to be in any pain. Her mind barrier had disappeared, but he still could not read her thoughts. Yet he couldn't leave her alone, and he needed answers. His aunts needed them. The irony of this situation never failed to amaze him.

One could not obtain answers without using his heritage.

Using body transference, he found his Aunt Esther investigating trampled flower gardens. A white dusting covered the black petals.

"You're gardening and I'm dealing with the wrath of Council?" he asked in astonishment bordering on irritation.

"There's not much we can do now, except wait for the time to materialize. She can't enter our world quite yet." Esther waved her hand over the flowers, shaking her head.

He didn't want to know and found himself asking anyway, "What happened?"

The white dusting disappeared and the flowers straightened. "Mrs. Waters has difficulty with teleportation."

He rolled his eyes, willing himself to not ask what she meant. "Why can't Cat enter? It would solve everyone's problems." Meaning his, and then he could find another place to be a hermit.

Esther dusted off her hands as she stood. "Your Aunt Marion could answer that better than I. Since she's not here, I don't know how to even begin, knowing you have always been frustrated with my way of explaining things." She gave him the "I told you so" look when he rolled his eyes and sighed. "You need to find the root of her power and release it. I don't know how, where, or when. All I know is we have forty-eight hours tops."

He did a double-take. "Forty-eight hours?" No one wanted to make this easy on him.

"Council's hit man has never failed to destroy a soul, and he is coming for your cat as we speak."

"Why the hell is everyone calling her my cat? I didn't lay claim to her."

Esther touched his shoulder, a worried look in her eyes. "Look. It's not easy. I know you loved her." He backed away, not wanting sympathy. "It was several hundred years ago. It's in the past and has nothing to do with today."

Marion appeared. "It has everything to do with the past. Your heritage. Who you are. You have the power to find the answers and somehow you are linked to your cat."

Damn it to hell, he thought, backing away, shaking his head. If they were going to talk about the past... "Do you remember when you were holding Katrina in your arms?"

"How can I forget when you bring it up?"

"You may have to repeat the past," Esther said.

This time he understood his Aunt Esther perfectly. "It killed her."

"She wasn't strong enough," Marion said. "I miss her, too, Dante, but Cat is stronger than Katrina. She grew up in a different environment. In Katrina's era, women were taken care of, considered weak, and were not taught to survive in a man's world except to be taken care of by a man. Cat's soul is fighting to stay alive, and the energy flow is trying to connect with you. Take advantage of it and don't waste time."

Marion waved her hand and Dante found himself back with Cat. His cat.

The affection rising for her couldn't be pushed aside or what he was going to have to do. He had tried so hard to save Katrina and it had backfired. Still, Cat was not coming out of the energy-induced coma, and he would have to connect with her energy source to fix it.

He sat beside her. "Cat, if you can hear me, don't hate me for what I'm about to do," he said, surprised that he meant it.

He focused on finding her strongest energy surge and followed it, ignoring the pounding of her heart.

Or was it his?

Chapter Eleven

Jack hated Lycon's little piece of paradise.

Paradise was the extreme opposite of what Lycon's world really represented. It may look white and calming, but once one looked a little higher, it was too late to escape. Death was the only way out of Lycon's personal hell playground. Jack never heeled for anyone and hated coming here, but in order to keep Lycon off his playground, Jack patronized Lycon's place to give progress reports on the death contracts.

In this particular instance, Cat's and Dante's.

Lycon never went to anyone. They came to him. It was almost as if Lycon thought he was safe as long as he didn't venture out of his comfort zone, which explained why he hired others to do his dirty work.

When Jack died, his soul had disintegrated into a million pieces. Lycon must have scoured the universe for every miniscule particle of energy to raise him from the dead. Jack knew it wasn't completely his soul or he would not revel in this sadistic madness. A part of him almost made him want to ask Lycon if he had donated pieces of his own soul to bring him back.

He left that for another time and another battle.

A man screamed from high above. Other men and women hung across the room. Some unconscious and bloody. Others staring with horror as Lycon approached, palm out, his energy bursting towards the screaming man, searing the flesh open. The man's soul oozed from the tiny invasion to a small drip into a special container.

Jack cringed, quickly masking his distaste. He had a feeling Lycon was working on a little soul DNA exploration. He may enjoy a little terrorizing here and there, but there was a major part of his soul that forbade him to act in the extremes.

Lycon stopped and the man had breathed a sigh of relief too quickly. Lycon blasted the man's body and his soul poured out until there wasn't a drop left. In a matter seconds, the body exploded, leaving no residue behind. Lycon floated towards the others and stopped as if realizing he had an audience.

Jack had learned early on that Lycon was a sadistic soul from birth and the younger brother from hell. A brother he refused to acknowledge as a brother. Family by blood. No matter how many times their mother wished Lycon's soul to be purified after being reborn over and over, it came back worse. Jack's soul was dead to his kind after Dante had destroyed it, but he sure as hell didn't want to be brought back by Lycon.

"Is there a reason you couldn't trust me to fulfill my contract my way?" Jack asked.

Lycon was working near the ceiling and descended toward Jack, his white robe and long white hair as deceptive as the world he controlled. Lycon stopped short of touching the ground, choosing to hover rather than plant his feet directly on it.

"I never take chances with family." Lycon held out his hand and a drink materialized. "You were drafted, not a volunteer, my brother. Must I remind you of the clause in our contract?"

Jack's eyes focused on the drink and sent it crashing against the wall. He remembered the clause in the contract. If Cat died by someone's hand other than his, Lycon's clause stated Jack had failed to deliver, despite the death was a death. "If you want this job done right, don't make it harder than it needs to be." As he turned to leave, "Why do you want Dante's cat?" He knew full well why, but he wanted Lycon to openly admit he was Cat's father.

Lycon's face hardened. "I want what is mine."

Jack knew his brother was heading towards a major meltdown

when it looked he had put his finger in a light socket, his hair billowing out.

It was time for Jack to placate or disappear. And as he made it a rule to never placate, he disappeared.

Jack planned to be the fly on the wall next time he wanted to find answers. Why did Lycon want Cat killed their way? If she wasn't one of them, why not use a knife? For now, it was in his best interests to give Dante and his cat time to dig deeper into her past, which would shed answers on his little brother's obsession with her.

Everyone left a trademark identifying himself. Lycon was noted for master takeovers and mind control. Jack's specialty were the bombs he built. And Dante's were multiple, never fully targeted. Dante's family was as old as Jack's—both were of royalty and like minds in peace; then, their worlds were destroyed by an entity, still unknown to this day.

Jack's father blamed him for the destruction and hadn't spoken to him since, but his mother had believed differently. Jack had an idea who might've been involved, and he would continue to do a little digging of his own until he could prove his innocence and see who was treading on dangerous territory.

His territory.

Chapter Twelve

Dante realized it was her heart pounding. Not his. He was not a praying man, but he would do anything to have Cat back spitting with attitude. Focusing on the strongest energy surge he could find, he used it as a guide, willing his body to keep the absorption of her overflow from him until he knew more.

The glow of light faded and everything went black.

Her body jerked and he was swept forward, out of control. The beating of her heart grew louder. He struggled to regain control and found the current too strong. Loud echoes of air rushing in and stopping immediately came at rapid intervals. Her body jerked several more times, tossing him through the darkness until he was thrown at a wall. Pain racked his body.

All was quiet. Too quiet.

He felt himself lifted and slammed against the wall over and over with rapid thrusts.

The pounding came with less frequency. A wind brushed his arm quickly before disappearing and returning. The roar of the surge was obliterating his focus. The currents slamming him against the wall suddenly decreased. It wasn't much, but enough for him to realize she was having seizures, unable to breathe.

He had limited the use of his powers within her body, not wanting to harm her. It was a damned if he did and damned if he didn't choice. Holding her energy surges at bay, he opened his mind and saw what he had been slammed against and laughed. He was in for a rocky road.

Her mind was layered with multiple auras, activated to resemble barriers, unless one was invited inside. He had heard of the tales from his aunts and how it could cost one's soul, because once another is invited in, it was for a lifetime. He probed the first layer. Thick. Black. It was easy to pierce the shell. The next wasn't that simple. Gray and cloudy but more difficult to slice through. His mind scanned for a break or sliver of a tear. None were seen. His power told him to blast through. After several tries of rushing and slamming into the wall, it dissolved.

The last aura hinted of its vulnerability, easy accessibility in the white sheath protecting her. He slammed through and was almost kicked out of her mind completely. A surge of energy came from behind and blasting him into the white sheath. He tried to counter the attacks and found the power surges stronger.

Cat, you need to take down the barriers. Whatever is behind them is drawing these energy surges to attack.

She didn't respond.

Using his sight, he found her lungs struggling to expand, the weight of her energy crushing them. The only way he could eliminate the surges and help her survive was to destroy her mind barrier.

He flexed his hands and cradled her face, seeping his energy inside. Focusing his mind, he entered her body with his sight and faced her stubborn mind barrier.

Her energy retreated.

He demanded its return.

The energy surge rose to a tidal wave but did not attack. As he aimed, the energy surge mimicked.

The energy surge was not trying to destroy him.

It was using him to eliminate her barrier. Bolts of power flew from his hands as he sent them crashing into the wall. The energy surge hit after him. They attacked over and over. He stopped and inspected the wall. There was a small crack, and judging by the age of it, it had been made a few days ago.

Suddenly he was hit by a wave of energy. He didn't push it away. He accepted its power. He threw his mind, his power blasts, combined with the energy hitting in unison, at the crack. Her body shook and a piece of her wall crumbled.

Echoes of heart beats and lungs struggled to breathe.

Speaking to her energy surge, he asked for more. It gave. Between them they threw everything at the wall, pounding at it until there was silence. The echoes and breathing had ceased. The energy surge died. A roar spiraled through her body, and he realized it was going to explode. While he had control, he left her body.

She was not breathing or moving, her face ashen. He listened and found a slight heartbeat and placed a hand on her rib cage. He saw her lungs were not functioning. Focusing, a light grew beneath his hand and forced her lungs to inflate and deflate. Her heart pumped every few seconds.

He waited, closing his eyes, willing her to breathe.

Nothing happened.

It could not happen again. Whether or not he wanted to admit it, the situation was demanding he admit his growing affection and chemistry with Cat.

His lips flattened, willing himself to not destroy everything within his path and forced her lungs to work.

He waited.

Nothing happened.

No sass, no violet eyes glaring at him for destroying her barrier—he knew he had failed. It was only a matter of time before her heart would silence forever. Lifting her into his arms, he wrapped the blanket more securely around her limp body. He did not release her and held her close, wanting her to feel she was not alone when her heart beat one last time.

His aunts were right. Cat had been stronger than Katrina, fighting for her life longer and harder. He was at fault—he had realized too late her energy source had been calling out to him, asking for help in destroying the barriers she had erected.

The time between heartbeats had doubled.

He had not been able to read her mind or release her energy source to her soul in time. The powers of her soul had knowledge and control of its own strength until each person connected with it, and if contained much longer, she would explode from the rising energy.

In her final moments, her energy had tried saving her.

Her body rose slightly from his arms and then went limp, falling back.

The heartbeat struggled to prolong its final beat.

He held her tight. She would never understand how much she had chinked his armor. He would go to his aunts and ask if he could bury her at Lake Hope. If her soul had survived, he wanted it protected by the purity of their world.

He leaned to say goodbye. As he brushed a kiss across her lips, a hint of her energy slipped through. He accepted the last part of Cat and breathed a part of him back into her with one last kiss. There was no room for sadness until he knew her soul was safe. He pushed his emotions back in his heart and allowed anger to replace it.

She was too young to die. Why hadn't her family warned her? Explained what was needed in order to harness it safely? The cruelty of Jack, or whoever contracted his services, to push her source to reveal itself had been too much pressure for her to handle. She had not known erecting multiple barriers would increase the determination of her powers to be unlocked, willing her body to unbind them.

The heat of his anger surged within him, and he sent a bolt towards the wall, blasting a hole in it. He could feel the rage begging to be released but banked it. He needed to get Cat's soul out of here without being destroyed.

He bent to pick her up and found violet eyes staring up at him.

"If my grandmother were alive," Cat said, her voice raspy. "She would be turning over in her grave with holes in her walls." As she spoke, a hue of golden energy escaped her lips with each breath.

She smiled when he didn't answer. "Ahhh, it is true. Cats *can* take tongues."

His answer was to cover her mouth and kiss her thoroughly, taking her energy, attitude, making it his.

His cat.

His woman.

His protection.

And now, he would show her what her family had not.

How to channel her energy until her powers fully unleashed. Show her what his heart felt.

As she returned his kiss, surprising him by slipping her tongue inside, her hands touched, feeling her way back to this world and to what lay between them. Little by little, he felt her strength return.

Chapter Thirteen

Cat followed the smell of food to the kitchen after changing into her pajama bottoms, tank top, and a flannel shirt. Her mouth watered at the tossed salad with fresh tomatoes, red onions, parmesan cheese and freshly made croutons on the table. Dante set a sliced loaf of French bread next to it and stoked the fire with a few logs, glancing pointedly at her bare feet.

She shrugged, not feeling cold.

He carried a bowl of piping hot stew to the table, sat across from her, and waited silently.

"Hmmm … a cook, too," she said. "Surprised some woman hasn't snatched you up."

He cocked his head and gave her a look that clearly said not to step foot near the subject, no matter how light-hearted it was. "Eat before it gets cold. Next time, put some socks on."

She didn't have to look down to see socks had materialized on her feet. "I had to get dressed the old-fashioned way, but you nod and socks cover my feet? You were holding out on me."

"You're not freaking out at any of this. Why?" He put down his fork, passed her the bread and took one for himself. When she refused the stew, not feeling very hungry, he ignored her and dished out a small helping. "You need to keep up your strength. I have seen many things in my life, and the funny thing is, you haven't been shocked from the moment we met."

She took a few bites to please him, then for herself, each bite savory. Unable to remember the last time she had eaten, she finished what he had dished out. She hadn't realized until now that he had finished and was waiting patiently for answers, his back against the wall.

Two could play at that, she thought. "I see you require food just like me."

"I eat, sleep, drink. I'm like you." *In every way.*

The side of her mouth went up, not fighting his presence in her mind. "Point taken."

Not yet.

The clasp disappeared and her hair fell past her shoulders.

It was him.

His eyes darkened with intent. A subtle caress followed the curve of her ear. She fought the whisper of need rising inside. The bold smile knew she was affected. Dared her to deny it. She bit her lip as his mouth caressed her neck. He moved to the curve of shoulder and traced the bare skin above the line of the tank, dipping under the strap, the flannel shirt sliding off with the strap. A kiss grazed her bare shoulder. Her eyes closed. Her shoulders went back as she tried to hide her expression. Her lips were unable to silence her moan from his mind.

"Point taken," she whispered and regretted voicing it, wishing she had waited to see how far he would have taken his point.

Your energy has chosen me. We are bonded for life whether you or I accept it. I have forsaken my heritage for centuries. I became a hermit on Earth, separating from all that I have known, making a new life for myself.

From my family. My world. The drama.

The pain.

And the pleasure.

But no more.

He pushed the tank strap on her shoulder and placed the flannel shirt back in place.

I have seen the destruction. Seen it first-hand with someone I had loved. Felt the last heartbeat as she died in my arms, but not until after I had done the ultimate, and I had not even bonded with her. It was not enough to save her. Katrina. She had snatched me up. Stolen my heart, made me feel. Taught me what it is to be happy, to love,

and in the end, mourn. Family obligations brought me back to my
heritage, reminding me to protect those protecting the innocent.
Souls of purity. Power.
I learned there is no way of eliminating evil completely, only
harnessing it to decrease its destruction.
If these souls are destroyed, the world will be at the mercy of Council.
There is no running away from one's past or destiny.
And destiny has dragged me back into the world of feeling by a
little cat who is more than she realizes.

Cat's eyes snapped open, and she lost her breath in the strength
of his determination and arms as he lifted her up and headed to
the bedroom. As Dante laid her on the bed, his hands gentle,
caring, she read his mind for the first time.

It was a victory for him.

She nearly came as she saw the pleasure she would experience.

"You will definitely know what it is to bond completely, but
first, you need sleep before we hunt for answers." He shook his head
as he joined her, pulling her into his arms and covering them up.
"What you saw *will* happen after we find the answers to unleash
your powers and find out why someone wants you dead or alive."

"Look. I am not expecting anything from you. If you are gone
tomorrow, at least I have a head start on staying alive." She snuggled
against him, needing human touch. If she were really honest with
herself, she needed him. She'd been on the run, alone, forcing the
terror so deep below the surface, hoping she wouldn't lose her mind.
It was pure heaven having a reprieve to lean on him.

When he left, she would be alone. "You can believe what you
want, but you've been a bachelor for centuries, and you will crave
your independence. Habits are hard to break," she whispered.

He touched her forehead and her eyes closed. "Sleep well, my
little cat."

The last thought she read was something about "hell freezing
over."

Chapter Fourteen

Jack sat at the bar and ordered a draft beer. What made him think he could come into this establishment and brainstorm the puzzle pieces? The taverns of yesterday were perfect for quenching his thirst, his eyes, body, and mind.

Those days were long gone, and it never ceased to amaze him how many times he had forgotten.

He thanked the bartender for the beer and grabbed the frosty mug. The barmaids of today wore men's pants and their shirts emphasized their endowments, leaving little to the imagination.

Multiple televisions mounted all around the room, games in the corner, games in each booth, and loud music. His mind sought a reprieve. He lifted the mug and quenched his thirst.

At least one out of three wasn't bad.

Despite the distraction of today's technology, he finished his beer and ordered another. Whatever secrets Lycon guarded about Cat were buried deeper than the year of his birth. Every favor Jack called in brought dead ends past Cat being Lycon's daughter. Not one snitch had lied to him. They were bound by ethics of their kind—honor among thieves—to tell the truth.

Well Jack wasn't without his own secrets.

One he shared with no one, except the only woman who had stolen his heart.

There was a possibility he could use it to break free of Lycon's control. He had one shot and one shot only. If he missed, nothing would sever the ties to Lycon.

A familiar scent took him back in time to innocence and love.

A group of woman chatted as they passed behind him. One of the women laughed.

His heart clenched in pain.

He turned his bar stool at an angle, longing to hear it again.

There was no chance of her soul existing.

He pulled his mug into his hand and lifted it, searching the tables, but he found no connection and turned.

The beautiful, haunting laughter called to his heart once again.

He whipped around.

In the corner booth sat six women in their twenties and thirties, drinking margaritas and beer. Their waitress brought their orders. The girls passed around the small plates and dug in. They were all beautiful in their own way, yet none like the woman in his heart. A woman's hand, her face concealed, snatched the last onion ring.

Ah, he had missed this one.

She did not lean forward and show her face. The waitress came back with another round of drinks. The woman's slender hands reached for the mug, cradling the bottom of the dark ale with one hand.

His memory liked her ale dark, always reaching for it in the same way.

Her hands stilled as if she sensed eyes upon them. The woman leaned back, her hair black as a raven, long and thick. Her face turned, and it sucked his breath from him. She scouted the area with a casual air about her, and when she spotted him, she froze.

It couldn't be her. She was dead. Her soul destroyed beyond repair.

Her lips trembled. The doe eyes became thoughtful and tears welled up. She turned back to the group when someone touched her shoulder.

How was that possible? No soul could be raised from the dead.

The woman leaned back again and shook her head, sensing his need for answers. Later, her eyes said.

Jack turned, hiding his hate as he nursed his beer.

Dante had a lot to answer for.

Chapter Fifteen

Cat snuggled closer as he caressed her hair from her face, whispering, "Time to wake up. I can feel his presence nearing."

What were the odds of waking up and this past year being a bad dream?

"I wish," Dante said. "I will fix you breakfast, and we will search the house for answers. I'm sure this house has secrets in its walls." He hooked a leg over her as she rolled to get up. "No morning kiss?"

She smiled, avoiding him. "Time to get up."

"Touché." He pulled on his jeans, leaving the button unsnapped.

She lay on the edge of the bed, propping her head with hand, admiring the view. His muscular legs and taut buttocks definitely showed those jeans off well.

"Finished?" he asked, his voice husky with underlying need to finish what he had started last night.

Laughing, she sat up. He had a body she would never get tired of seeing—if he stayed.

"There is no *if*, Cat."

"I didn't—"

He turned around and held her chin, his thumb stroking her lower lip as he bent to kiss her. "You cannot block your thoughts from me anymore. Remember?"

She grinned. "So, if I wanted to tell you—"

He shot her a dark look. "Not happening in this lifetime. You won't be able to say 'no.' Last night proved it."

She breathed deeply, remembering quite well.

Stretching her arms and yawning, she wished for a dark, bold cup of coffee to wake her up. She was going to need the caffeine.

A mug materialized in her hands, smelling suspiciously of one of her favorite haunt's brew. She sipped tentatively and sighed. It was. Coffee was right up there on the list with a man like Dante.

*

After breakfast, she finished dressing, turning down his humorous offer to dress her his way. Their way. She decided to start with the living room and tucked her legs under as she sat in the middle of the living room on the braided rug. Her grandmother had reasons for keeping the cabin for more than a hideaway for her.

But why?

Would she have revealed Cat's heritage? Power? Had she known of the trouble in her future?

There was nothing in this cabin except the bare necessities. Her grandmother didn't believe in shopping for the sake of it, so how much was there to really look at? A bedroom, kitchen, bathroom, and living room. No cellar, attic, upstairs, or basement. Not one family picture of her parents, her grandfather, any cousins—that she knew of—or of her and her grandmother. She had been enrolled in a private school of one hundred kids from various cities. The kids lived in foster homes while away from their families during the school year. Cat had been lucky and went home every day after school.

There was nothing under the couch or bench. There were no cupboards in the kitchen except an empty pantry and a block table for an island to prepare food. The stove was for baking and heating. The bathroom housed a claw tub, basin, and a commode, keeping permits and a paper trail to a minimum. A small windmill created electricity on the necessities her grandmother refused to do without. Now Cat knew why. She grinned. Lips pursed, she racked her brain for anything out of the ordinary. Her grandmother would never have hidden anything important outside of the cabin. She checked under the bed frame and mattress. Unloaded the blankets from the trunk older than time itself as her grandmother used to say. No false compartments. None of the rooms held a hidden safe.

She sagged against the door frame, missing her grandmother.

Why had her grandmother been so secretive? The only friends Cat had been allowed to play with were the ones from the private school. Her grandmother had said she knew all their families and they were safe, which explained a lot, now that she thought of it.

The front door opened and Dante stepped inside. "What's wrong?" He closed the door, studying her carefully. "Find anything?"

She shook her head and closed her eyes, hoping to stop the chaos and the tears. It was hard knowing so little about her life, and the pain was still fresh from losing her grandmother. The sound of his boots gave him away. She willed the tears away, but it was so hard when the man was strong enough to take on the world, saved her life and, was standing his ground with her.

She did what any normal girl would do.

She went into his arms and burst into tears.

He held her for a long time, letting her cry it out on his shirt. "Listen, you have every right to cry. I'd give you more time and make you forget this past year, but we have to find answers fast. He's outside the property lines, testing the safeguards." He wiped her tears with his thumb. "Can I look into your mind?"

She nodded.

He kissed her forehead before heading into memories of Cat's childhood and the present. "You've looked everywhere and nothing. Is there anything you want to keep if this place is destroyed?"

"Grandmother was never one for knickknacks, photos, or jewelry." Cat bit her lip, looking around the room, afraid this last connection to her grandmother would no longer be standing.

She spied the shadow box on the wall, hidden by shadows. As long as she could remember, the light never hit that part of the wall. and her grandmother always forbid her to touch the ancient relics. Her grandmother had said they could not be replaced.

"What is it?" Dante's sight tunneled onto the grounds and into the air, checking for danger.

She pointed to the shadow box. He lifted it from the wall and carried it into the kitchen and set it on the block island. She ran her fingers over the box seeking a hidden lock, hinges, or sliding compartment. There were none. The window was clouded by age and film. If they broke the window, it could destroy the clue they needed.

Biting her lip, she looked at him. She couldn't help but wish this day were an ordinary day. He was quick with the comebacks, called her bluff, and he was hot eye candy. She wanted time to explore him without the darkness baiting them.

Cocking his head, he sighed, apparently ignoring her thoughts. "What?"

She couldn't help but laugh. The short time they'd been together, they had become very comfortable being around each other. "I need you to do something." Brows raised, he crooked a smile. "Can your mind get inside this box?"

He laughed outright. "Never thought you'd ask." He sought an entrance. "Strange." He moved closer, touching the object as he tried again. "It's not letting me in." Circling his hands around the box, a burst of light shot into the box.

The box remained intact.

"I have never had a problem with objects before." He paced the floor, stopped, drummed his hands on the cabinet and paced again. "It can't be." He turned and looked at her, his facial expression grim. "I should've guessed."

"Guessed what?" she asked.

"You. The shadow box. Our heritage." He shook his head. "I hope you're ready."

She backed up, shaking her head slowly, biting her lip, afraid to ask. "Ready for what?"

Palms on the block table, he smiled. "Your first lesson."

She hissed inward, sensing she had the upper hand for the moment, and met him at the table. "How about a little trade?" She stood on her tip-toes, flashing him a sexy smile. His eyes raked her body and mind. She grew warm.

He laughed, tilting her chin upward as he raised her body off the ground, bringing her face to face with him. His tongue traced her mouth possessively. Breathless, she allowed him full reign. The heat of his silent promises were powerful and consuming. She caught the uncensored thought slipping into her mind.

He wished her sweet mouth was not so addicting.

She deliberately parted her lips more, offering him a taste. His hand held the back of her neck as his addiction overrode his hesitation. His mouth devoured, taking what she offered willingly. Shaking, she raised her hands and placed them on his chest, to steady her emotions from flying so high, but they never reached him. He continued to push her higher and higher, forcing her to accept his lead and power. Her lips felt cold. She opened her eyes, frustrated that his lips were no longer demanding, seducing. Wanting to pull him closer, to have him finish what he started, she found her hands locked under his, holding the shadow box.

She hissed, her body aching at the need rising within her.

Don't think. Summon your energy and direct it to your hands.

Holding her hands in place with his mind, his hands grabbed the back of her head as his mouth demanded her attention. He was not gentle or seductive in stroking her mind to come, to feel, to fly. She wanted to feel all of him, not just his hands and thoughts. Wanted to strip his clothes off and run her hands and mouth over him. To taste and seduce his senses until he forgot everything but cumming in her mouth as she devoured him, making him lose control. Her breasts were full and aching at the thought of his tongue circling her nipples, suckling.

Suddenly his mouth covered one breast, stroking it as he kneaded the other with his hand. He switched, placing the other in his mouth, giving equal attention before searing kisses on her throat, whispering that he could smell the heat of her dripping where he wanted to plunge inside as he bent her over, naked and willing, screaming his name.

Now, he roared, forcing his power through to aid her energy.

She screamed his name, unable to shake him out of her mind, wanting to release her body from this need to have him thrust slow and hard through the heat pooling between her legs, the pain unbearable from having been denied so long.

It was too much.

Cat, do not think. Let me in.

Her hips sought his, knowing he was out of reach. She moaned from the heat, the slick sensation from the wetness dripping beyond her control. Her swollen feminine core throbbed as he diluted her common sense, whispering to her energy, her mind, and the fires within her soul.

"I understand the battle of the heat. I promise, it will be easier for you to accept me completely. The harder you fight me, the higher you will fly and longer it takes to quench the fires building from the pit of your soul to your sweet liquid pooling, begging for release. I will have what's decreed by our laws.

"I will accept your tongue licking me dry, the rushing heat to your mouth will never end, making me cry out for you. My body is never shy but wanton when you are near, begging for you to take me. I can't stop my body from needing you, but I will refuse this. It is too much."

Dante made his decision.

Her mind read his refusal, his determination. She cried out as he entered, the energy rushed to his will, understanding the necessity to strengthen and unleash her soul. She could feel the strength as his power slid inside. He accepted the challenge of teasing her into submission as he conquered her denial like a man riding a horse fresh from the wilds. Her body shook with force from the energy, the light, the power roaring in her mind, through her body. It scared the hell out of her.

She tried to shove the box from her hands.

To end it.

His mind was stronger, unrelenting in its seduction. The demand to release her energy and embrace her heritage would be denied no longer.

She cried out his name as the energy released, bursting through, realizing it wasn't the only thing he had released without being inside of her. This man was too dangerous if he could make her cum with words and thoughts.

Chapter Sixteen

Cat couldn't stop shaking. Couldn't open her eyes or move. Dante released her hands and moved behind her, lowering her body to the ground. He wrapped his arms around her from behind and held tight.

"I'm here. I'm not letting go," he whispered, the pain in his voice as evident as he was hard, straining to be inside of her.

The strength in his arms allowed her to lean on him.

To give her time to think.

Right now, her mind barely held a coherent thought. She took a deep breath, held it and exhaled, fighting for some semblance of control. She tilted her head back against his chest.

No matter how fantastic of a ride that had been, she would not attempt that again.

His hand smoothed her hair from her face. "There's more to come. It only gets better and never ends."

"Don't ever do that without forewarning me." She sensed his amusement as he tightened his arms around her.

"You two are not going to do that within my hearing again," an elderly woman's voice chastised.

Dante tensed at the mocking voice.

Cat forced her eyes open and stared in shock.

An image floated above the small crystal hanging from the chain. "Do you know how long it's been for me?" Catherine, Cat's grandmother, said sternly. Her grandmother's white hair was longer, softer. "I may be ancient and dead, thanks to—never mind that now—but I can still remember. Cat, don't you dare cry."

Cat wiped the tears with the back of her hand. "I don't understand."

Catherine held her hand up. "I made a promise to your mother, and I kept most of it, until my untimely death, damn him." Ignoring Dante's silent questions, she continued. "I don't have much time, because you're about to have a visitor. There are more like you and Dante. We kept our children in small communities to prevent us from becoming extinct. Safety in togetherness. Our world was destroyed, and we scattered to the Earth, a similar world to our own. Later, we heard a new world had emerged and there was hope for a peaceful ending. We decided to crossover in small numbers. For many, it was a mistake and, for those of us still on Earth, we learned it was more dangerous to crossover when word spread of the original Council members Lycon followers murdered."

Dante released Cat to move closer, his expression warning her not to touch or they could lose the image of her grandmother.

Sadness passed over Catherine's face. "Your mother never told me your father's name, but she handed you over, made me promise to raise you in our ways when the time was right. I'm sorry I waited too long. I wanted to protect you, but, in the end, it almost killed you. It was rumored you were destined to unite with great power. A power so great, when fully combined, you will save the new world." Tears streamed down Catherine's face as she studied her granddaughter, no longer hiding her sadness. "We are depending on you to embrace your heritage to the fullest. I love you, and we will see each other again. Make me proud, Cat." Catherine's image faltered, shimmering in and out. "I am going to break a promise to your mother and tell you she is—"

Cat cried out, lunging to stop her grandmother's image from fading.

Dante held her back. "She's gone," he said, grabbing the crystal and clasping it around her neck. A quick glance told them the shadow box was empty and it was dark outside. "We have to get out of here. He's almost through."

"How?"

"No time to explain. We have to follow the trail. My aunts will be waiting for us on the other side. I sent a telepathic message that it is time. I'm not willing to risk teleporting with you. If we are attacked, there's a chance I could lose you. We will have to run for it." He sighed at her expression, his own mirroring hers. "I'm sorry, Cat. We have to burn the cabin. We don't have time to look for any more clues, and we can't afford to leave any behind."

She held back when he grabbed her hand and snapped his fingers. The bedroom filled with smoke and flames. She cried out, stopping him as he snapped his fingers again, but it was too late. The couch and braided rug quickly sparked into flames, engulfing the room.

She relaxed her mind, following what he had shown earlier and aimed her hand. He quickly intercepted and swung her over shoulder, ignoring her demands to let her down.

"So help me, Dante, I am going to kick your—"

"Later," he said, dodging trees and low branches, running toward the path.

The cabin's roof shot sparks into the air. Wood crackled, covering the sounds of his boots as he ran. Within minutes of his setting the fire, the cabin was completely engulfed in flames, lighting the moonless night. Glass shattered and a wall dropped, taking part of the roof.

Fury took over Cat and she tried summoning her powers.

"You summon your powers now and all hell will break loose. You can't keep it submerged as long as you have, release it, and still expect to have complete control," he warned. She didn't care. "Damnit, Cat." He swatted her behind. "Do you want him to find you? You are inviting death."

"Put me down," she demanded, heeding his warning for the moment.

"No. I know the locations of the safeguards."

Her mind was going in all different directions. Her body wanted the passion Dante ignited. Wanted to explore his body into the wee hours of the morning. Yet, there the man stalking her, the deaths and supernatural occurrences would be forever in their lives if she stayed with him.

A man like Dante would not be easy to walk away from for so many reasons.

The second she had a chance to sneak away, she would.

They passed a rusty shed and the corn husker. Dodged the old boarded well. He was like a machine, keeping up the extreme pace. They were close to the path and the bridge crossing over river. He would have to put her down as the bridge would not hold both of them, and then she would disappear. She saw the outline of the bridge, but he didn't stop.

"It's too deep to walk across. We need to take the bridge," she warned, hearing the roar of the river from the recent rainfall.

He didn't heed her words.

It wasn't even close to dawn. She supported her body with her hands on his shoulder and looked up. He wasn't slowing down. On the other side of the river, a white light emerged from the sky and grew. He shifted and jumped. There was no way they would make it safely.

The raging river below foamed with white suds. The sky was eerie, silent and black as hell despite the white glow in the distance.

"We're not going to make it," she screamed, unable to stop watching their fall to death.

Their descent was steady. A sudden shift upward, and a black shadow swept under. It was difficult to see what had flown under them. They began to descend towards the ground. As his boot touched, he broke into a dead run, twisting and turning as black shadows dived at them. She didn't scream, didn't want to break his concentration, not knowing if the shadows were real.

From her world or his.

She had to stop thinking of this world as hers.

She was not fully human.

A hard object rammed them, and she went flying from his arms. She reached for him and missed, hitting the ground hard and rolling fast towards the river. She dug her fingers into the soil, attempting to gain control.

Someone shoved her backwards, pushing her down the steep embankment.

She flipped and rolled towards the river; her only saving grace was if she could latch onto the tree stump. Her last thought was the irony of having powers within and not being able to avoid plunging into the river.

Chapter Seventeen

Dante raised his hand to bring Cat back to him, but he was kicked to the ground. He whipped the knife from his boot, arcing it outward as Jack flew into the air, his knife aimed for the soul.

Dante countered with a blast and threw his knife, aiming low.

The knife stopped in mid-air, flipped over, and speared towards Cat.

Dante focused on the knife and changed its direction. A jagged bolt of lightning hit Dante, knocking out his line of vision, and the knife returned to its original course.

Jack sent Cat sliding down the river embankment and lunged for Dante, missing him as Dante twisted and kicked him into the air.

Dante thought Jack was a run-of-the-mill killer, hired to take out Cat, but those eyes were prepared to destroy his soul and glowed as if they had been waiting a long time. "Who are you?"

Jack stopped in mid-air, hate and death radiating in his determination. "Don't recognize me, old friend? How can you not see the soul you called friend? The man who took what was mine?" Jack spiraled through the air, connecting with Dante's chest.

The impact sent Dante flying over the river and Cat's body below, her hand dipping in the river and her head muddy, oozing blood against the tree stump.

"We are evenly matched in powers, and you know it. Why are you after her?" Dante said, eyeing Cat's stability before lifting her into the air.

"You don't know?" Jack snarled, casting his hand in Cat's direction.

The old Jack was centuries in his past and dead.

Cat's body dropped to the mud, unconscious, barely missing the stump, sliding towards the river.

Dante sped towards her, but Jack beat him, suspended above Cat, aiding her body dangerously to the edge of the swirling, murky water. Jack blocked Dante's attempts to pull her to safety, the pull of nature's gravity and Jack's thwarts against Dante were stronger. Cat's long hair dipped into the water, as her body remained suspended, waiting to ride the angry currents. Jack waved his hand and the water pushed and pulled. Cat's body dipped lower with each pull as the water rose to suck her in.

Dante had to buy time. "It was not me. I was still your friend that day. The same friend matched with you in the dark alleys to sharpen wits and strength." Their families had settled in the same vicinity when their worlds had been destroyed.

"You don't remember, do you?" Jack waved his hand, giving Cat a nudge until her forehead was submerged in the water.

Dante raced towards her.

Jack raised his brows, his hand aimed to push her in the moment Dante moved another muscle.

Dante stepped back.

"You may not remember, but at least your wits haven't dimmed," Jack taunted.

The water rose, churning hard to pull her in, wanting a sacrifice.

Dante's heart lurched. "She's an innocent party. Who wants her dead?"

"My soul is tainted; as you well know, our souls are not guaranteed when shredded to tiny little pieces. I assure you, I am as strong, if not stronger."

"I was not the one who destroyed your soul." Dante had aimed for the shadow behind Jack.

Jack snarled, "Throughout the centuries it has been said, 'A picture is worth a thousand words.' So, let's have a look at what happened, shall we?" One hand still on Cat, Jack's other hand projected from his soul into the sky, taking care to keep Cat in his grasp.

Two young men came out of the men's club, both a little inebriated, their pockets, if Dante suspected correctly, lined fuller than when they had entered. They walked past several establishments before turning right into the dark alley. Simultaneously, they took their dinner jackets and laid them on the ground. Next, off came the ascot ties and top hats. The men rose into the pitch black sky, above the clouds, their faces hard to distinguish, yet the hard strength of their powers and bodies were not. Power emerged, lighting the sky like fireworks.

Dante and Jack laughed unwillingly, remembering the good days.

"Damned shirts buttoning in the back. The generations following us keep taking us backward. We're heading towards the seventies again. So help me," Jack was the first to speak, nodding towards the projection. "If someone brings that time period back in, I will do that contract for free."

Dante chuckled. "That one I will help you with. My parents forced me to dress without using my powers. Do you remember when the town referred to our fisticuffs as lightning? We would've been burned at the stake if they'd caught us."

Jack would fight at the mere mention of his violet eyes. They were no longer that color but dark and vengeful. The last time he had seen Jack was the night—

Another projection formed and a young, curvaceous woman lay in Dante's arms. Her blue evening gown mud were splattered, her ringlets drooping around her slender pale face. Blood seeped into the already formed puddles in the alley. An evening coat lay across the woman to protect her from the rain while she waited for help. She was trying to form words, but a man laid a finger on her lips, telling her to save her breath. To fight to stay alive. The last words she uttered before the bobbies came were replayed to both men: "I love you." White light shot to the left.

Dante had never forgotten those words and hoped to never hear those words at a time like that again.

Nor had he seen who had destroyed his friend's soul from the shadows of long ago.

Dante speared through the sky, meeting Jack face to face, blocking him from Cat.

"Doesn't look good, does it?" Jack said, sneering at the bloodied body below. "I lost the woman I loved to you. Lost those words to *your* ears. *Your* heart. They were mine!" Jack gave a right cross, decking Dante.

"You only heard part of it, Jack." Dante came back at Jack, grabbing him by the shirt with fists. "Those words were for you."

"You lie, dog!"

"Damnit, Jack. Stop this contract now, before it's too late. She is not part of our past. If Katrina were alive, I could prove it. Sadly, she is not."

Jack cast Dante backward with a wave and shot to the sky. He kicked Cat into the river, his laughter maniacal as Dante speared into the water, following her rapidly sinking body.

The water churned with wild tenacity, taking whatever sacrifices came its way.

Jack shot at a nearby dark cloud before he vanished.

The rain was hard and relentless from the first drop. Dante dove into the water, seeking his Cat. His mind could not get a fix on her energy. It was as if it had died.

She had died.

The water was rising too fast and the currents were too strong, ready to suck Cat in at anytime. If he could slow it down, it might help.

Would it be too late?

Dante? We are here.

We can help.

He heard his Aunt Marion and Aunt Esther speaking to him. What could they do that he couldn't?

You have made us old before our time.

Ten orbs floated into the darkness of night and pouring rain, transforming to ten shadows. Those ten shadows became his Aunt Marion, Aunt Esther, and their friends. They spread apart, unmindful of the rain soaking their white robes, and raised their hands in the air.

The rain slowly ceased. Mud settled to the bottom of the river. Tree bark, limbs, and stumps rolled onto the embankment. White foam dissipated.

Still no sign of Cat.

The water will clear, and you will be able to summon her energy. It will call out to you.

The water cleared, none too soon for his peace of mind, and his soul summoned her energy, seeking any sign of life. A white light, resembling a rope, bobbed from the other side of the river, wrapped around a tree branch embedded in the mud. He focused on the rope, lifting it toward him, but the rope held strong despite the strength of his power. Her body was not surfacing. The rope was not responding to him. Using his sight was useless as it could not see through the murky depths still intertwined with Jack's darkness he left behind.

The link to his sources alerted him that Council's hounds were closing in fast.

Time had run out.

He would not give up.

The link had leaked word of Cat as the answer to protecting the new world, and he would not leave without her. His mind refused to bow to his heart and declare he was doing this for family obligation. Once his obligation had been met, his hunger satisfied for the woman whose soul had latched onto his, bonding him to her for eternity, he would disappear.

He dove in the water, swimming below the surface searching for the branch and white rope.

It was his only hope.

Treading water, he scouted the sides of the embankment and saw logs and debris sifted from the churning water lying in the mud. He dove under, but not before a large object broke loose from the embankment and resurfaced.

A log, thick with mud, followed the current's pace, barely missing him.

Turning back to his search, he dove, but his body refused to move, forcing him to tread water.

He commanded the release.

His soul burned, clenched in agony, longing for the light.

He fought the pull on his heart, soul, and mind, compelled by the water's mystery of darkness, ignoring his commands.

A warning set off in his mind link.

Darkness was minutes away.

And hell was not far behind.

Even in the black of the night, hell above and darkness below, if his soul had not disobeyed, he would not have seen it, believed it, or recognized it.

Barely bobbing in the water, the glowing was latched onto the branch. He found his body released from captivity and followed it until he reached the branch, grasping it with one hand and capturing the glowing rope with the other. In that instant, he discovered it was not a rope, but her soul going against everything he had ever seen and linking itself to the branch. He let go of the branch and using a hand-over-hand method, he found her face down, camouflaged by the mud, the water desperately wanting to finish her off. He jumped out of the water, pulling her into the crook of his arm as he lay beside her.

She was not breathing.

Placing his hand on her heart, he felt the barest of heartbeats. Her hair was caked with mud, not one strand spared, the weight heavy to his touch as he moved it from her face. Her face would never need a mud treatment again. His hand upon her chest, he summoned her energy to her lungs and, combined with his power, expelled the water. She turned in his arms, choking. Her eyes fluttered as she gave him a weak smile. She reached for his face, but her hand did not make it as she passed out.

At least she was alive.

Chapter Eighteen

There's no time. Bring her now, Dante. Marion's telepathic message seeped into his mind, unable to ignore her warnings any longer.

He lifted Cat, knowing it wasn't Jack who was hot on their heels. Dante had not recognized any cruelty in Jack during their years of friendship. Any soul associated with evil was recognized early on in life. Not one ounce of hate or killing instinct had lived in Jack's soul. He may have been serious, but *that* Jack knew how to cut loose once in awhile and had a sense of humor.

This Jack had seen hell one too many times.

Dante shifted to jump.

His Aunt Marion stopped him, joining Esther and eight of their friends. *Do it the human way . Whenever any sliver of our heritage, our power, is used, Council thrives on the scent like a dog in heat and can hone into our location.* She waved him back.

He didn't make it far.

The river swirled, foaming at the top as it sucked the tree stumps and branches back into its murky depths.

You couldn't wait until we were across?

There wasn't time. They are seconds away. He knew Esther's patience was thin for a change, worried Marion was taking too much on. The shadows had transformed to their orbed state. Now only she and Marion stood outside their haven. *Don't jump across. Every second saves everything we've worked hard for. We will wait as long as we can.* Esther stepped with Marion into the light.

Now they told him.

They had all wasted precious seconds without this knowledge.

The bridge was too far away for his peace of mind.

He felt her stirring from within, then her hand pushed at his chest. Heard the unspoken words to let her down so she could run. In her weakened state, they wouldn't make it. He touched her forehead, forcing her back to unconsciousness. If nothing else, she wouldn't feel a thing if they didn't make it. A much easier death compared what would happen if Council caught up, for Council was not known for its mercy. A black haze stormed like an army, ready to leave no survivors.

Head tucked low, he struggled to stay on the bridge as the wind pounded at his body. It clawed his arms, threatening to sweep Cat from his arms in an inhumane way. The roar of anger, loud and harsh, came from the haze like trumpeters announcing the promise of endless pain.

She stirred.

He fought the wind. Ignored the roars.

The bridge began to shake. The sides tipped high and long, alternating from side to side. One end fell into the river.

A few more feet and they would be across, though not safe.

Not until they made it into the light.

We must leave. They are too close. If we leave, you and Cat may be safe. They think it is us and have honed in on the scent of our powers. We will never be out of communication range. There will be another time that is right. Once we have left, wait for the heathen darkness to subside—only then will it be safe enough to get ahead of them.

Just because they were right didn't mean he had to like it.

The light ahead vanished, leaving no shred of humanity or hope.

Total darkness and impending death hovered, seeking to touch the light.

To extinguish it for eternity.

As if sensing meatier prey, the black haze snarled and dipped towards the bridge.

Protecting her from its sight, he shielded her with his body, crouching low.

The black haze hesitated, backed up, and disappeared as if it had been a bad dream.

He knew better. They had precious seconds to get out of here before hell swallowed them whole, chewing them from the inside out. He had survived centuries. Cat wouldn't last another five minutes. Taking chances were all they had left, and it was better to die taking a chance than to die in Council's hands.

The night swallowed them whole.

The river stopped churning. The water cleared, debris free. Large rocks appeared downstream like large stepping stones to safety. The bridge fully connected. Water trickled ankle deep. The wind calmed. Wisps of smoke curled through the cool air, tempting those near the burning embers to seek its warmth.

*

Dante strode through the portal into his home. The electricity had not been turned off since he had left to fulfill family obligations. As far as he knew, no one had reported him dead. Many thought of him as a loner. Eccentric.

He'd need that warmth to help Cat after being submerged in the river. They no longer had the cabin to hide in; Jack's arrival had taken care of that haven. For now, his home would serve their purpose until it no longer was safe. If Jack had wanted him dead, he would have found this place and attacked him already. Teleporting with her was a risk he had been willing to take, considering the odds. He was not sure if she would be in his arms when they walked through, but they had made it together.

The lights flicked on, their beams low, guiding, adding warmth to the air as he made his way upstairs. He had to laugh at the irony of his destiny. There was only one way into his home, but many ways out. Apparently his soul had guided him with the building plans, watching out for that day when Dante's past and future connected.

For the day when Cat needed him most.

The door swung open as his boot hit the top step. She wasn't going to like this decision taken out of her hands, but tough. Even soaking wet, she didn't weigh enough to take anyone down. Her wet clothes disappeared. He dried her body and hair, and mentally produced warm pajamas to cover her body. He walked over and the covers drew back, hoping she would gain the strength to make it through whatever she would need to stay alive before it was too late.

And that meant unleashing her powers completely.

He would do it with or without her help.

Laying her gently on the bed, he pulled the covers over her still body. He had done what he could with her body, but the next twenty-four hours with her soul were crucial.

Hopefully, there will be enough time for her to heal properly.

He brought the large chair over and sat next to her, putting his feet on the edge of the bed. Without searching the house, he knew it was empty of his past and full of human hardware. No personal items. It lacked individuality, any sense of emotion, friends, business accomplishments. It did not lack showmanship, money, status. Every detail was planned by a well-known decorator from the intricate carvings in the woodwork by an upcoming sculptor to the elaborate kitchen he never used. This home, his life, his business—it was all empty.

He did not like being reminded by such a small thing as his heart.

In a normal life, in normal times, he could see this house warming up with her soul.

The way she smiled, laughed, gave him a hard time made him want that life.

Want more.

As much as he would like to avoid what was to come, to have a normal life, to have a lover sleeping in his bed, wrapped in his arms, he couldn't dare think past keeping her alive.

Dropping his feet to the floor, he didn't fight the urge to touch her, smoothing the pale cheeks, checking her forehead for a temperature and changes in her pupils. Her vital signs were on target. Breathing regulated. She was still alive, her soul intact.

If he wanted to keep it that way, he had to connect fully with his world and make his stand loud and clear.

There was one person who had a three-way connection with his aunts, Lycon, and Earth.

Jeremiah.

Two people knew Jeremiah best, or at least how to get a message to him.

Keeping a mind link open to his Aunt Esther only, he reached out.

It's about time. Already ahead of you. Jeremiah will be contacting you. Not sure when or how, but I would make sure there is an open invitation to receive him. Now I need to take care of Mrs. Waters. We've created a national stir over the Sahara Desert. Maybe we can relocate it to California's forest fire or the five states going through a drought. Too many places to choose from, and time is limited. Until we get rid of it, it leaves a trail wide open for Council.

He wasn't sure if she was shaking her head from Mrs. Waters' situation or him.

Dante? Don't wait so long next time. Marion, please ask Mrs. Waters to let me have the honor of relocating the lake. Talk to you later.

He did not have patience in waiting for Jeremiah to reach him. There was so little time.

"Esther and Marion were right," a voice said coming from the hall.

Chapter Nineteen

Dante whipped his hand to blast but halted immediately, sensing the safeguard between them. He didn't want Cat hurt any more than she was. "You sure as hell better be Jeremiah."

Jeremiah's attitude spoke volumes as he lounged in the doorway. He was good at what he did and knew it was an extreme bargaining chip if he was ever captured by Council. "The one and only. Sorry, didn't give you enough time to let me in. I couldn't help but pick the safeguard." His youthful looks didn't look sorry. "Love a good challenge." He arched a brow and waited.

Dante waved him in.

Jeremiah waved his hand and the safeguard disappeared. He gave a nod toward Cat as he entered. "I see you found each other."

"She found me." Dante eyed Jeremiah. The guy stood six feet tall and looked wet behind the ears.

Jeremiah laughed robustly. "I'm three centuries old. That hardly qualifies me as wet behind the ears. I didn't know she was destined to be yours or I would've called you." At Dante's quick jerk of the head, he continued. "I pulled her to safety. I believe she told you about it. If Esther and Marion had asked me to locate you, I would've found you in within a day.

"But they didn't ask. And it wasn't my business to offer. Besides, have you ever tried offering to help women who aren't ready? Never touch that with a ten-foot pole, my friend."

"You're hell on wheels, aren't you?" Dante couldn't help but like Jeremiah.

"And the hottest commodity on the Lycon market, I hear." Jeremiah held up his hand. "No need for explanations. Seen and heard it all from Esther earlier. You want a direct link. No problem. Let me enter the power source within you and Cat, and you will have it."

Dante wasn't about to trust this guy explicitly even if his aunts did. "I'm sure you are extremely talented to hook anyone up to the direct link without the aid of my power source."

Jeremiah hooked an index finger on the curtains, parting the silky material and peered out. "You're right." He turned and walked to the end of the bed, his expression was of regret. "It is my price for linking you to that direct line."

"I'm limited on patience and time. Explain."

A whiskey appeared in their hands.

Jeremiah raised his glass to Dante. "Salude." He threw his head back and downed it, his long blond hair loose and wild. "It's actually a gift to our people to keep the numbers level with, if not higher, than Council's. I made a mistake and it cost me dearly." His glass disappeared. "Jack has been commissioned to take Cat prisoner if possible, or kill her to stop her powers from being unleashed. You two are already bonded by your scent, but that does not guarantee her safety. If she is taken prisoner, what I'm about to do will enable you to track her down."

Dante did not trust his own family, much less a stranger. This Jeremiah looked like a renegade in worn jeans, shirt, and scuffed boots, on the run and out for his own take. .

"It is my price. Take it or leave it," Jeremiah said bluntly at Dante's hesitation. "I choose to look this way because I blend in. You know we all have the ability to be luggage free."

Damn this mind reading ability. But Dante needed that direct link to find the answers to stopping hell from chewing on their heels. "Agreed."

Jeremiah slipped in and out of Cat and Dante in seconds. "Finished. You have your hands full with this one." He smiled his condolences and congratulations. "She's a worthy soul mate."

Dante couldn't have said it better. "Yes, she is," he said, quietly.

He wished their future were different and he could disappear with her. Carefully, he again checked Cat's vital signs and pupils. All clear.

A chair materialized and Jeremiah sat down. "From my sources, Jack's hate has doubled since his brother revived his soul. Not sure how he accomplished that one, considering that when your soul is destroyed, it can never experience life again." He waved a hand in the air and two steak dinners appeared before them. "I'm starving," he said with a smile, cutting his rare steak and sighing at the first bite.

"What do you know about Jack and the contract?" Dante, too, sliced into his steak. It smelled like Singer's. "Somehow, I think there's a price on your head dead or alive having this much knowledge." He moaned his appreciation. Definitely Singer's. It had been years since he had visited that place. He felt guilty eating while Cat lay there, but he knew he had to keep up his strength. Their kind still ate and required nourishment like humans.

"She'll be coming out of it soon. I sensed a change in her energy level between the time I entered and left. She will know someone other than you has entered, and Cat will be unsheathing her claws for whoever allowed me in." As Jeremiah stood, the chair and empty plates vanished. "I don't want to be around. If you need me, I've added a link to contact me. There's also a silent binding contract between us: you cannot sell me out nor can I sell your connection to anyone. I value my reputation."

Jeremiah vanished.

Cat stirred.

Dante's blood and energy stirred with her movement, both wary and excited. It was better to be on defense than offense. He shifted and cast a protective safeguard, invisible to the eye, over her body.

Her violet eyes snapped open, and as luck would have it, Dante was the only one within her fury.

Cat struggled against the safeguard, furious. "Who the hell was in my body? I know I didn't give permission."

"I did."

Her eyes whipped his way. "Do you want to repeat that?"

Not really, he thought, but he was game as long as there was a safeguard between them. "Do you remember the guy who saved you from the van?" She nodded, not backing down from her fury. "He just left. I gave him permission to enter our bodies. It was the price he extracted to get the answers I needed."

She relaxed her body, but her eyes were still angry and accusing. "And do you think it was worth it?"

He was dead serious. "In a heartbeat. He was able to sense the changes within you on coming around and provided a way us to track each other if we are separated."

She closed her eyes and sighed. "Don't worry. I'm not going to kill either of you. Just yet. Do you mind?" Her hand gestured to the invisible safeguard.

It disappeared.

Her eyes opened, revealing nothing that was certainly going on in her closed mind. She stirred to her side and pushed up.

He was at her side immediately. "You need your rest."

"Where are we?" She ignored him, sitting up and wincing.

That was as far as he allowed her. "My place."

"Nice. You and my grandmother have very similar tastes in decorating. You both lack personal touches." Her hand flew immediately to the crystal around her neck.

Several pillows appeared at the headboard, and he scooted her back against them, surprised she let him. He made sure her legs were covered and sat down, preferring to pace the floor but chose to keep the energy within the room sedate until she was stronger. "How are you feeling?"

She gave a harsh laugh. "Like someone dragged me to the bottom of the river, hit my head on a stump, and used me as a little toy to bat around on an air hockey virtual reality table. You?"

"Worried about you."

"Don't sound so shocked. I'm having a hard time thinking I was worried about you. It doesn't seem real to have this happening so fast." She looked delighted at this observation. "Don't get me wrong, I'm not wanting you to be worried about me, but there's a bit of me that's happy I'm not alone in acclimating to everything," she said, her voice trailing off as she slid down into sleep again.

He was amazed she had stayed awake this long. Her vital signs were strong, but her mind, soul, and body were still weak. Her energy source stayed at bay as if it knew this was not the time to push her. His legs and mind felt the call to walk, anything to keep his mind focused, but he did not want to leave her alone unguarded. He brushed a kiss on her forehead and placed a protective safeguard around her. Making sure she was sound asleep, he walked downstairs, letting his mind wander.

His home was the only place he felt safe in doing so. The windows were many. Large. Light filled and welcoming. They allowed him to look out at the world as people lived, breathed, loved, and died while he chose to suspend his life, hiding. He had wished for his life to be like theirs. Normal. Instead, he could only pretend he had a normal life with a normal house with a large island granite countertops and chairs gracing its sleek line. The tile splash did nothing except emphasize the beauty of the cabinets and echo the emptiness of the life he had lived prior to Cat.

Four large round columns, strategically placed within the living room, and large comfortable furniture graced that empty room.

The fireplace blazed as he walked past.

Today was a day marking firsts.

Chapter Twenty

Jack didn't dare show up at the bar after tonight. Not if he planned on keeping Lycon's feelers to a minimum. Lycon pounced at the least bit of interest, and there would be no living with him. Jack would slit his own soul to avoid giving the man total control over him, having seen what lengths his brother employed to keep people.

Without freedom.

Without choice.

Without peace.

And peace of mind was a hot commodity these days.

Almost hotter than the man on Lycon's most wanted man: Jeremiah.

Lycon was never happy as a child and hated anyone who found life good. He had never played well with others, and when they learned what he was about, they left. Or tried. Mind control was Lycon's main skill and he used it effectively to stop them.

A frosty mug slid toward Jack.

Jack scowled as the bartender slid the dark ale his way.

The bartender wiped the counter and tipped his head towards the mug. "Some classy hottie came in earlier, paid a c-note for that beer, and left a message. Said you would know what it's about. If you don't mind my say'n, she had the most beautiful violet eyes. She said, 'Invite me in.'"

Jack's soul wrenched at those words.

Chapter Twenty-one

Cat woke to Dante scowling at her. "Do you want to tell me what I did wrong or did someone take your favorite toy?"

She knew she looked like the cat that had licked the cream, but she couldn't help it. Something about him made her want to give him a hard time.

His scowl deepened. "It's about time. You've been sleeping for thirty-six hours." His eyes devoured her from head to toe as if he couldn't get enough of her. "How do you feel?"

"I'm starving. Bored out of my mind. And feeling no pain. I'm craving a long, hot shower." She moved about the room, stretching her legs and warding off his protective instincts to catch her if she fell. "Is your bathroom that way?" she gestured at the adjoining door.

"Yes."

She cut him off at the door, slipping under his arm. "I can handle it from here. I'm no longer an invalid."

"Do you think a door is going to stop me?"

"No. I just like seeing your expression when I give you a hard time."

His laughter slipped through as she closed him on the other side.

She about crooned at the sight of his shower. It was large enough to hold six people, tiled in earth tones and encased in glass. Fresh towels and a wash cloth hung on the door. Quickly shedding her clothes, she stepped inside and turned the handle to red. It had been so long since she had the luxury of enjoying a hot shower. Water shot from jets on all sides, aimed low, easing the soreness in her hips and legs that she had hidden from Dante. Water fell from the large cap above like a beautiful tropical rainfall, soothing and refreshing to her mind.

There hadn't been one private moment since he found her climbing up the ladder at the hotel. It wasn't Dante making her wish for private moments. It was the madness. Burning down her grandmother's cabin, the attack, near death, and knowing it may never end. Her mother leaving her behind. The identity of her father kept from her.

All because of her damn heritage.

A heritage she wished like hell would never have been part of her future.

Maybe if she—

A wave of dizziness hit, forcing her to reach blindly for the tiled wall. The flow of blood and energy swept rapidly through her body. The roar of her energy flow pounded and demanded. Her knees buckled and she slipped, trying to hold onto anything until it passed. Her vision blurred from the war within her as it continued to take over her mind and soul. The roar grew louder. The heat within her veins and soul boiled, rushing for an escape.

Wishing it would end, she cried out.

Unable to take it any longer, she sank to her knees, shivering, holding her ears to stop the pounding.

She didn't sense the jet sprays taking her breath away, the water stopping, or Dante's arms wrapping around her shivering body. A hard wall supported her body, and she leaned towards the warmth, hoping it would stop this madness inside of her. She barely noticed being dried off and dressed in warm clothing. As the heat soaked through, the jolt to her heart brought her senses to the surface. For the first time, she noticed Dante as he lifted her into his arms, carrying her down a winding staircase.

"Kitchen or living room?" he asked.

"Living room," she murmured into the hard wall of his chest.

Too shaken to be freaked out by him taking charge, she didn't protest when he relinquish her but sat down with her still in his arms.

"Be thankful you were with me. Your soul is rebelling. It won't let you run away. Not when your soul chose mine. It needs what mine can give."

The images he shared mentally of the forgotten ancient stories, the myths of soul mates parting showed the madness overriding minds and souls.

The dark rumbling of his words made sense, but she wasn't ready to go deep just yet. "Distract me. Talk about you and Jack. The guy doesn't even know me, yet he wants me dead."

"Trust me. He has me at the top of that list." He stared into the fire, reflecting on the memories. "Jack and I were friends a long time ago. He had been somewhat of a loner when we met, but then so was I. It's become a part of our heritage these days to protect who we are. To preserve it for our children. Because we are spread all over this Earth, trusting anyone outside our families is daunting. We aren't sure of the risks." He shook his head with a quick laugh. "Thankfully, it was Jack who found me jumping from side to side and not my mother."

She looked up. "Every kid does that."

His laughter was deep, filled with warmth. "Little cat, I forget you have not fully embraced your heritage. I will provide more information for you. I was almost of age, still reining in my energy surges. Testing the boundaries, you might say." His eyes were no longer black but a rich shade of brown and she was trying hard not to let them eat her alive. "I was jumping from one building wall to another, high above the alley way. Just as I was taking one last jump to the rooftop, something caught my shirt at the scruff of the neck. I struggled for release and twisted. It was Jack. He had been suspended above me, watching the whole time. From then on, we helped hone each other's weaknesses and perfected our strengths."

"What happened?" She didn't want him to stop, wanting to know more about this man who made her heart flutter and senses wild. She hugged him, snuggling closer for warmth.

At least, that's the excuse she gave herself.

He stilled as if surprised by her affection, but continued, "Jack began courting a woman a few years later. She was beautiful and as untamable as her long, red ringlets that drove her nuts on a daily basis."

She squelched the rising jealousy over another woman in his heart, not understanding why it mattered so much. He had lived a long time and probably had many women in his time. "You sound as if you loved her."

"Everyone loved her. Women. Men. Children. Young and old." He smiled. "And I see the question you are not asking. Yes, me too. She had this inner beauty shining through, drawing people like a moth to candlelight. This inner beauty defied our heritage. We have always been a private lot after coming to Earth. She couldn't help but be friendly and inviting. Her parents loved Jack and trusted him to protect their daughter. They didn't see her death coming. None of us did." Some of the warmth died in his eyes.

"She died in front of us. Jack. Me. Her parents. Her soul had been pierced by a weapon not of that era on Earth. Our enemies had knowledge of that weapon, and it came into the hands of someone on Earth, because no one in our race would ever destroy a soul if they were of sound mind. Someone fired it into her soul and it exploded from within, tearing its purity, innocence, and light to shreds. She was unable to be healed, and her soul lost the chance to be reborn or reunite with a lost love. Jack and I weren't far behind her when she was hit, and I caught her in my arms as she died. Her last words were, 'I love you.'"

Now she understood why Jack hated Dante. "She had fallen for you?"

It was moments before he spoke, but whether pausing from this woman's death or the hate of an old friend she couldn't say. "No. She and Jack were soul mates yet to bond. Jack approached as she whispered the words of her heart in my ear. Words meant for Jack. She was afraid it would be too late to say them if she didn't do it right then. Only Jack didn't hear her request for me to pass those words to his ears. She died in my arms. Her family buried her and Jack disappeared, grief stricken and angry.

"There were so many things that needed to be said to clear up misunderstandings. Though, to be truthful, they were not his fault. Jack's love had been manipulated by a man who became infatuated with her, too. None of us saw it happening until it was too late."

"Jack wouldn't listen?"

"Men, no matter what world, react no differently. He was enraged at the loss of his soul mate. A soul mate he had been prepared to bond with for eternity. A marriage within our culture." He held her tight as she turned to discuss the last comment. "He wanted to lash out at anyone. And this infatuated person made reality even more difficult for Jack at a time when Jack should've had support from family and friends."

She settled back in his arms, fighting the urge to thread her fingers through his long hair just a fingertip away. "Jack doesn't see it that way?"

He nodded, stroking the back of her head to the tips of hair settled in the middle of her back. "Jack's perception is distorted on the way he died. Pieced together. His mother and I tried to explain, but Jack wouldn't listen. He cut off communication completely. Jack caught up with me four decades later and wanted to duel. I shot at a shadow behind Jack, protecting the friend I knew from long ago, but the shadow deflected it and my shot backfired. Jack's soul was mutilated beyond repair, and it died as he lay in his mother's arms. Whoever raised that soul probably holds the contract on you."

He lifted her chin. "We just have to figure out who it is, and we will find the answers on many gray areas," he said, his mouth a breath away from seducing her lips into submission. "I will try to answer your questions later." He stood with her in his arms and walked towards the fireplace. "For now, I plan to take full advantage of this night."

Chapter Twenty-two

The lights dimmed as two logs floated from the hearth into the fireplace. Wood crackled. Flames rose high into the chimney. Sparks rose from the burning embers, igniting more than heat as he lowered her to the floor, the soft plush rug cradling them. . The depths of his eyes, no longer a rich brown, were now fathomless and dark, intent on seducing her. His hands took over where the heat had begun to warm, drawing the heat from the inside out, forcing her to concentrate on keeping sane or lose control.

She had no intention of losing control.

She couldn't afford the price that went with it.

He rose above her, resting upon his palms, his mouth seconds from pulling her into center of the fire. *Stop fighting destiny. It is our heritage to embrace the power from within and the heat entwining our minds and bodies as one. Fighting it is useless. Invite me in.*

His tongue traced the seam of her lips, teasing, begging. Not waiting for submission, his tongue slipped inside as his mouth covered hers, refusing to turn down the heat. She let her head fall back, away from the heat.

Away from temptation.

Only she wasn't prepared for temptation to follow or the renewed determination of a man hell-bent on pulling her head first into the flames. His mouth went straight for the jugular, nipping and kissing along the curve of her neck, his hands holding her shoulders from dropping to the floor, encouraged by the breathless moans escaping her parted lips. She yearned to be warm from the inside out, hating the coldness seeping from the past into present. Her body ached to be near the fire, yet, her mind forced her body wiggle away. She needed to think of a plan.

A way out.

And she couldn't resist much longer. She quickly scooted away, but not before his hands trapped her hips from escaping too far. He was giving her an inch and refusing to let a mile part them by the look in his eyes. His hands slid her underneath him. He held her tight against the curve of his body, stroking the soft under curve of her breast.

She refused to give him the satisfaction of knowing he made her thoughts jump all around. *I can't. I don't know who I am or what is expected of me. My world is turned upside down, and now, you and my soul plan on turning me inside out. I need answers. You, at least, know your heritage. What the hell do I have?*

He flipped her and leaned over her. "I'll tell you what you have. You have your life. There's a power inside of you, begging to be released. A power that can save you from using all nine of your lives. Only you prefer to leash it until it bursts at the seams and orgasms into a tidal wave. There isn't time for a lesson plan or for you to be taught the rudiments of your heritage. The cold hard facts are this…" He cupped her face and hooked his leg over her body, preventing her from jumping up. "Your body and mind want all that it has to offer. Every. Last. Drop. Only you are afraid of your own shadow. When our children are born, they will know their heritage from day one and they will not be allowed to walk away from it."

Her heart skipped a beat at the thought of his children growing inside of her, but the idea of Jack and others like him trying to kill her stopped that thought cold.

She ignored his scowl, sensing he had read her mind. "Let's say you are right and we are married—not that I totally believe you—but with whatever nasty storm is coming our way, I refuse to bring children into this world." She poked her finger in his chest. "I am not afraid of my own shadow. It's the shadows wanting me dead that I'm afraid of. I intend to find out who they belong to. Even if

I have to die trying." She twisted out of his hold.

He growled, pinning her flat on her back, "Over my dead body. I have been patient in bringing you to your destiny."

"Whatever you're about to do, don't," she warned, placing her palm between them. "Time is limited." His smile infuriated her as much as it turned her on. They didn't have time for foreplay.

"You're right. We will have to do it our way."

"Our way? Don't you mean—" She stopped as the flames heated her toes, working its way up her ankles. There was something sensual about the way it touched through her socks, caressing. She rubbed her foot over the other. "What the—" And threw up her other hand out to stop him.

A burst of light streamed into his chest and sent Dante flying towards the ceiling.

The look on his face shocked her more than the power bursting from him. He stopped before he hit the ceiling, so she knew he could've stopped her and didn't.

"Whether you're ready or not, Cat, it's time to fly."

His expression of determination and the desire to finish mirrored in his eyes weakened her resolve to give in, knowing there was no place to hide from a man so intent on baring her soul.

Especially when she had invited him in.

"Is there any way we can stop this?" she whispered with longing, unsure of her own reasons for asking.

He descended downward, undressing her his way.

Her pajama bottoms slowly disappeared from the ankle up until there was nothing left of her bottoms. She backed up and held the material of her pajama top at her thighs, realizing she wore nothing underneath. His omission, of course, when he'd dressed her earlier.

"You're not answering me," she whispered.

He advanced.

She edged back, knowing there would be no reprieve this time. Not from her own emotions. Not from him taking her to the highest point and free-falling, a thought that made her shiver. It was freaky that something so wonderful could be so right. She held the material tighter, understanding it was for her own peace of mind and nothing would stop him.

Her collar slowly disappeared.. The bottom of her top slowly vanished. She attempted to grab both ends, not ready to give into the final joining, because there would be no going back.

She was afraid she would lose sight of finding answers.

"You're not going to give up until there's nothing left to grab onto. So, it's up to me," he answered, nodding to the last shred of material as it vanished from her grasp, "to get you to that point. Since you aren't about to undress me with the ways of the old, I will do it for you."

Cat could have run, but she didn't, and she wouldn't lie to herself any longer that it was her soul rooting her to this spot when his clothes disappeared faster than he taken hers, leaving nothing to the imagination. She shuddered, the need to feel his body on her overwhelming as his pants dissolved into thin air, revealing muscular legs. Trying hard not to stare at the well-defined chest and biceps when his shirt vanished, she could not ignore her inner feelings, the total attraction. Dante was a man primed as a warrior, trained to withstand any battle.

"Come to me." His eyes warned he was prepared to do whatever it took to unleash her soul, and nothing could compare to his warrior determination standing before her.

She backed a few steps, more for her pride than to walk away, because there was no doubt in her mind, she would not get away. "I need time to think," she said, shaking her head.

All around him the room shimmered. The fire, the fireplace, the couch, the stairs—it all faded away.

"You want traditional courting." He no longer smiled, his

mouth flattened with resolve, standing before her in a flash, reaching for her. "With what is at stake, it can't be done."

She avoided him and ran.

She didn't dare look over her shoulder or he would see into the windows of her soul. A place she had not looked for days, not wanting to admit what he declared, her body declared, for this moment. Her foot faltered on the only exit to refuge, the lip of the first step fading beneath.

Her soul refused to accept weakness as an excuse.

Curiosity forbade her to ignore what was behind her.

There were precious seconds to waste before there was nothing left.

Heaven help her—she was about to waste them.

She looked at the step fading inward and then towards the scent of fate in the body of a man high above her. He was so intent on saving her soul, sealing their heritage for all eternity.

He was safety and wickedness all in one body.

There was no in between with this man. Not his smile, his intent, his kiss, or the way his hands touches her every curve.

He would protect his heritage, his family, and his only soul.

A soul, come heaven or hell, bonding her to him.

She was not ready to relinquish power over her body or her soul. If it came down to it, she would fight fire with fire.

The only way a woman knew how.

The last step faded and as she lunged for the door, it, too, vanished, taking the bedroom door and the last exit away from reach. There was only one direction left. Fate, destiny, and desire had banded together in controlling the outcome whether she wanted it or not. She understood what he meant on strengthening two souls bound for one common cause.

Preserving their heritage.

At any cost.

It wasn't his need to preserve their heritage scaring the hell out of her but the thoughts he was sending to her of how fast he intended to take her to the highest point and free fall. He did not hide how enticing he found her legs as she flew to each step, barely catching them before each one faded underneath as her feet touched the next one.

"Your stubbornness turns me on. I welcome the challenge," he said, watching carefully.

He drove her to distraction merely by fluctuating between telepathy and spoken thoughts.

You have the curves that mean a man would never forget he is holding a woman. Curves and fight a man would kill over if another touched.

She leaped for the landing and found it gone. Clutching for the railing to stop her fall, she found air and screamed, spiraling to the floor.

He dove and swooped under, catching her.

She blushed as he let her legs slide down his body. Her nipples hardened touching his bare skin. She never dreamed the desire to have him inside could hit her so hard, so fast.

She almost creamed instantly when his eyes hardened and his words matched.

"I warned you there is no escaping."

And then he captured her mouth, sealing her fate and her reply as he tasted sweet surrender.

Her leg curled around his the moment his mouth set out to taste every curve of her body while his hands kneaded her breasts. She couldn't stop her sharp intake of breath or the moan filling his mouth as he sought to conquer, tweaking the hard nipple. He switched to the other, giving equal consideration. His mouth covered the first breast and she bucked, frantic to find release as he refused to let it forget the heat pulsating through her body. Her moans elicited a mental picture of his pleasure at the control over her. He suckled on the tight bud before scraping his teeth along the nipple.

He switched to the other, drawing the fullness into his mouth and she cried out, her back arching, driving her leg higher to his waist. His hands held her bottom and yanked it close, showing her this was real and destiny was a matter of time. She could feel the wetness slide down her other leg, driving the heat higher and higher. She was tempted him to wrap both legs around him to pull her into the flames.

Wrapping his hands tightly around her hair, it felt as though he were fighting himself from losing control.

"You are so beautiful," he whispered.

"There is one way to fight fire." Her words husky and inviting.

He pulled her away, searching her face for the meaning behind her words. His body jerked in response as her hand slid to do a little teasing of her own.

Hoping he would lose control before she did.

"You set this fire out of control, Cat. You may not be able to take the heat."

His hand cupped her swollen folds, palming with undulated motions, stroking the heat to a frenzy, fingers parted the folds, hesitating at her clit. Her head dropped to his shoulder and she began to pant, unable to stop. He pushed in a little, adding a second finger, moving at the entrance, teasing. Her leg dropped and he immediately brought it back up, holding it tightly in place, continuing the circular motion. Her hips sought relief, rubbing against his hand, seeking to push him in. The ache was rising hard and fast, and she could feel her cum drenching his fingers. She needed release soon, unable to take the heat much longer.

"Please." He was killing her. She pulled away and he dragged her back, her hips rocking in response to his touch.

He plunged his fingers in, waited, and slid them out slowly.

She cried out, "Now. I need you to take me."

He plunged two fingers deep inside, holding her hips in place as she bucked. Slowly sliding his fingers out, he plunged hard and fast, over and over. She panted against him, thinking of ways to take him out of control. Instantly, he grasped her by the hips and placed her over his erection. He held her above, forcing her to look at him and then drove hard, agreeing with her body of leaving foreplay to the wayside as she rode him, meeting his thrusts.

The room went black. Lightning streaked. Torrential rains let loose.

She screamed his name.

Chapter Twenty-three

Jack tensed, not from the two souls joining in the distance, because the joining was unstoppable after fate had made its decision. He tensed from Lycon's feelers snaking through the universe. Lycon had this uncanny ability to sense anything out of balance in his own little world. If Jack's world were soon to be destroyed, he, too, would be watching for any sign to squash like a bug, but since the love of his life had died, he had nothing to lose and nothing to gain.

Dangerous combination for anyone tempted to see where Jack's loyalty lay.

Jack was grateful invisibility was a part of his soul, blending him into the night to seek the peace of mind he thought he had lost for eternity. Every night he waited to see if she returned. This particular sports bar was the most familiar of his past.

Their past.

She would return sooner or later.

He had not invited her in as she had asked, wondering if a past invitation needed to be repeated.

The doors burst open before the greeter could hold them open for the guests exiting. They were loud, boisterous, and having a grand time. A few patrons stood outside smoking, waiting to be summoned. Out of the shadows, a woman appeared through the haze of the evening, looking high and low as if expecting someone to be lurking. He looked around to see who it was and when his heart pounded, recognizing her before his eyes, he realized she might be seeking him.

He looked closer and knew it wasn't him she was seeking.

For he would never have put fear into those beautiful violet eyes.

The scent of it was too far into the background for him to put a name to it. If he had, they would be annihilated, drawing Lycon's feelers breathing down his neck.

Following her inside, he waited for her mind to reach out to his. There was silence.

No answer to the worry or fear hiding behind the strength of those beautiful violet eyes.

His soul reminded him, he wasn't whole.

Wasn't the same soul she had invited long ago, which meant she was of pure energy.

Not evil. If her soul were blackened, tainted by evil, he would have no problem reading her mind. His soul reminded him of another tale, one that must be true: If one were tainted, in order for a pure soul to reach his mind, he must be do the inviting.

He wasn't sure he was ready for it.

What if it jeopardized her or his plan?

Would the same tradition follow of joining them together? Would he blacken her soul, or worse, draw the wrath of Lycon upon her?

He allowed himself to sit beside her, unnoticed. To smell the clean scent of her soul. To wish for death upon this blackness in his own. This raw despair washed over him as his mind remembered bathing her in the dead of night, wanting to prolong the joining until they could no longer deny it. His soul wished they could travel through time to prevent the future.

The quick turning of her head alerted him that she had sensed the old Jack.

But wasn't the old Jack destroyed forever?

She waved her hand over the napkin and writing appeared as quickly as it disappeared.

Invite me in before it is too late.

He wanted to reach out and touch. To remember what it felt like to touch purity. Then he recognized the foolishness of what life had dealt. Passion. Love. Betrayal. And death. *Ahhh, love. It is too late. I am following the path of no return, saddened by the state of knowing I had not sensed your return.*

And he wouldn't have sensed her return. Not if they hadn't completed the joining of their souls.

Second chances never came around.

His heart skipped a beat when her hand dropped to the counter and a tear fell.

He couldn't do it.

It wasn't fair.

To either of them.

He wanted to a hint of believing that second chances could happen.

Before he vanished to finish out his contract, he couldn't help but lay his hand over hers.

And sent an invitation the only way he knew how in this day and age.

*

A few minutes later, the bartender held out the dark ale. He waited until she accepted it her usual way, then slid her a napkin. "I delivered your message to the gentleman. He sends his love," he told her.

"That's all?"

The bartender smiled and wiped the counter carefully. "Only that the door is open for my soul mate of yesterday."

Katrina sipped the ale, thinking of another year.

Another century, to be exact.

She owned her past with a vengeance, including revenge for the man who claimed to have loved her and left her to die. The man her soul loved as no other left a void in her heart. She knew the love of her life had thought her dead for eternity, so she did not blame him for not staying for her family to piece her together. Part of her was grateful he hadn't.

For if he had, he would've seen the mirror image she had been about to reveal, jeopardizing all of their lives.

Instead, she used this mirror image as leverage to save all of them.

Now it was about to unravel a lifetime of deceit.

There was hope, she thought wistfully. If this Jack had any tiny connection left to her old Jack, then there was hope for all of them. She had one chance to make her move as a woman, as a lover for old time's sake, and join her soul to the man she still loved, if he was still alive—if she wanted to save her baby.

Their baby.

Finishing her ale, she went outside to the dark alley and jumped to the roof, blending in with the night.

There he sat.

"Hello, Jack."

"Hello, luv." He stayed at the other end until her tears fell, unable to stop the flow of the past from shifting through her heart and soul. "Don't cry." She leaned into his hand as he held her face with great tenderness and wiped away her tears.

"I can't help it. I thought you were dead forever." She so wanted to turn back the hands of time, erase the pain and devastation. "When I first felt you near , I didn't dare believe, but I took a chance and left a message at the bar for you. Please don't hate me."

"Shhh, luv. I could never hate you." He put an index finger on her lips as she spoke. "Let's not talk about the past. Not yet, anyway. I want to feel. Just this night. Before hell breaks loose."

The old Jack kissed her, pulling every emotion and light to the surface. She had no regrets for what she was about to do.

She only hoped she had enough time to explain why before it was too late and he did find a reason to hate her.

Jack pushed every thought of the past, present and future from her mind as he took over, piercing her soul as his tongue swept in and took over, ravishing her mouth with the hunger of a dying man.

Chapter Twenty-four

Dante sensed her questions and hugged her closer under the blankets. "Go ahead and ask. You won't sleep until you do." He snapped his finger and the lights went out.

"It's not a question. I don't know how to put it." Cat twirled her finger on his chest with an absentmindedness that hid her true thoughts.

From everyone but him.

If she had been raised and educated their way, she would understand completely. "You need some light shed upon what happened earlier." She nodded, laying her head on his shoulder.

The best way he knew how to explain it was to liken it to a similar tradition. "It's like … it's like two people deciding to get married. The bride walks down the aisle and after they say 'I do,' they are joined in holy matrimony by a priest or pastor. They are considered 'one.' The night of their honeymoon, they complete the ceremony by making love. They are husband and wife until death, and if they are lucky, they find love again should that happen. Only for us, the joining of our souls was forever, and there can never be another to take our soul mate's place. Everything fading, the lightning, the rain completed the ceremony of our two souls. If we are separated, our souls will find one another in the darkness unless death takes our bodies, and then we will have to be patient until our souls are reunited.

"It's like our parents. Prior to separating from our parents we are able to hear their voices. When we complete the separation, we have matured enough to block them out 'til the day we need them. There is always a bond between child and parents—*if* those two parents are joined in our traditional way."

She raised her chin and rested it on his chest, her fingers stilling. "There is the possibility of my soul, or yours, being obliterated like Jack and your lady friend."

He refused to look in that direction. "True. After a joining, a couple is stronger, tougher to break apart."

"I don't remember hearing my parents' voices."

"Then they would not have completed the joining."

"What's next?" She raised her eyes, smiling up at him, obviously reading his thought. "Besides *that?*"

He would make up for it later. "We need to bring all your skills to the surface and hone the one sending me across the room." He did not include that her energy provided a preview seconds before her energy sent him flying. A warrior must always be one step ahead in protecting those he loved. Energy always forewarned others of impending dangers—even new skills of one's mate.

"We do have time on our side in this. When two souls have joined, their knowledge, power, and skills are transferred to their mate. In time, the experience will follow."

"I know my parents are no longer around, but if they had joined, would you be able to hear their voices or call out to them?"

"I don't know. This situation isn't heard of happening often. Why? Are you hearing voices?" He slid his hand down her backside and curled around her bottom, loving the feel of her close by his side.

He had never thought of settling down, and had thrown a royal fit at fulfilling family obligations, but now, if anyone touched one hair of his mate, he would hunt them down and destroy them.

She had lain her head back down. "No. Just curious." She yawned. "Sorry. I'm so sleepy."

"It's okay. You're going to need your rest." He held her until she was fast asleep.

Dante had placed feelers of his own out there on her stalkers. Jack wasn't the only one. She didn't know he had seen the part of David's, her ex-fiancé, obsession and murderous intent to rid Cat of her family. No one knew where David's lair had moved, but Dante had received word of a new lead from one of Jeremiah's pigeons who had requested a meeting tonight. Placing the seals up for protection, he vanished after leaving Cat a note of his meeting, ordering her to stay put where it was safe.

Lightning streaked through the sky as he teleported to his meeting. A quiet rain followed, sharing news of another joining.

*

Dante waited on the beach for two hours longer than he anticipated. Impatient for his pigeon to show. He didn't like leaving Cat alone without having full use of her power. It was a warm summer's night here and the tropical breeze was pleasant, despite the pitch black sky. He had nothing to aid his sight unless he wanted to shout his location to Council by using magic.

He trusted Jeremiah explicitly, because his aunts trusted Jeremiah with their lives. Jeremiah liked using many pigeons for everyone's safety and had recommended this guy, marking him dependable and secure. Someone must have taken him out or he would have arrived long ago.

A piercing light flashed before his eyes. Pain radiated throughout his body, spearing his mind and soul, forcing him to the ground.

A shadow crossed over his face. "I will take good care of your mate. She'll need a little consoling. We have dealt with loss before and will get through it again."

The shadow kicked Dante's hand away and a tiny trickle of a glow streamed from Dante's body into the sky.

"Thanks to our technology, your soul will lead me to her. Her father will reward me handsomely for her safe return." The shadow laughed. "After I'm finished breaking her in the rest of the way, of course. Thank you for educating her. You've made my life a little easier." The shadow disappeared into the night.

Dante knew he was alone or his soul would have alerted him now that it had a slight scent of the shadow. He had been away from his heritage too long and had grown soft in checking every avenue in safety. That shadow was as old as he to remain undetected when he had arrived.

The cool breeze didn't soften the pain as his soul left his body. There wouldn't be anything left to say goodbye to Cat. If he called out to her, the psychic trail would lead death and evil to her faster than the death to his soul.

He had never dreamed he would find his soul mate, much less join with her.

Focusing on the memories of when he'd met Cat kept him from succumbing to death completely. His body racked with a fit of coughing and he twisted over enough to turn his head to the sand and spit out the pooling blood.

He wasn't sure if he could summon a telepathic message through the universe to his in-laws, but it was his last hope.

"You just had to go and marry my daughter didn't you, Dante?"

Dante was seeing a ghost.

"No. You're not seeing a ghost. I heard through the grapevine you and my daughter were destined as soul mates. God help you when her father learns who married Cat," Katrina said.

Dante's body racked with another fit of coughing, wanting to laugh at fate. He nearly passed out from the pain. "Who's her father?"

"It's not fair to tell you before he knows." Dante felt the searing heat to the surface of his soul. "I've made a temporary fix on your seal to your soul. The only person who can repair it completely is my daughter. Luckily for you, since you're my son-in-law, my spies forewarned me of this attack." She levitated him, aiding him to stand and wrapped her arm around his shoulders. "Show me the way, Macbeth, before you pass out."

"You're never going to let me live it down for trying to set you up with him. I should warn you—she knows of you, just not your name or face. For that matter, I didn't know you were her mother until now." Dante stumbled, hating to lean on her for strength.

"Do men ever learn? Never talk of another woman to a woman. She's going to be jealous as hell and want to kick my ass and yours when she sees me. Not to mention, I screwed up as a mother, leaving her with mine to raise her. I thought I had done the right thing and learned it wasn't," she said with a remorseful laugh. "It only delayed the inevitable war."

"Don't remind me. I believe we both forgot destiny and fate cannot be ordered around. I don't want to be the bearer of bad news, but did you know about your mother's death?"

She flashed the portal door to standby. Her body tensed and her lips flat lined as her teeth bit it. "When? How?"

"Months ago. Murdered." He sent images to her mind. His body and mind were ready to give out. "I hate to say this, but if we don't go now, you're going to find the way to my place on your own."

The murderous rage in her eyes spelled a death warrant for the shadow named David.

The same shadow that most likely ambushed him and stalked his Cat.

Chapter Twenty-five

David was not a patient man. It had taken every ounce of humanity he had stolen and perfected to blend in with this world to wait for the opportunity to steal the light from the new world rising. He had heard of Dante's aunts and other rebels taking a stand against darkness.

Although that dark world was not of his making, it was a stand he would not allow.

From the first moment he had seen Cat, he had been obsessed with bringing her to his side to rule his side of the darkness. He had been willing to bring her grandmother, too, if it meant gaining Cat. But her grandmother's aura wasn't buried like Cat's. Catherine had seen the black devastation and sent him a telepathic message to walk away from Cat. Hers was a light that would destroy him once his back was turned.

He couldn't.

Hadn't.

As much he enjoyed killing the old woman, he felt an emotion he had never experienced.

Remorse for the pain he caused Cat.

That emotion would not be allowed ever again, but judging by its strength even in his darkness, he could only imagine how she would rock his world if she turned from the light.

David followed the traces of Dante's soul from a distance. He had killed a few souls in his time to stop them from ruling his darkness and knew there were no guarantees on a soul's reaction once it was released to die.

The trail stopped outside of a ten-thousand-square-foot home surrounded by black steel gates with multiple security systems protecting the property against unwelcome humans.

He placed his hand on the gate. The energy on the seals made his human flesh want to sink below the ground until it could no longer be touched by the light.

He stepped back, unprepared for the immense power of these seals.

Seals warning others not of this world.

Detonated to kill anyone to take what was Dante's.

David didn't blame him.

She was in there.

He could feel the purity of her light.

Rumors of her destiny to join with Dante had spread far and wide, revealing once her powers were unleashed completely, they could annihilate any hint of darkness. It didn't matter that Dante had succeeded in joining with Cat. The end game of turning Cat to darkness was more important, and he had plenty of time to make sure it happened.

Now that Dante was out of the way.

David's patience was nearly exhausted, but the wait was almost over.

The remains of Dante's soul seemed to sniff out the seals. It hovered by the gate, and a portal doorway opened a seal small enough for the remains to shift through. David had mere seconds to shapeshift and ride on the tail of Dante's remains. He breathed a sigh of relief when the seal accepted him. There were more seals to break, but it could happen if Cat worked with him.

Chapter Twenty-six

Cat paced the floor. The burning in the pit of her soul had not stopped since she had awakened alone, and it grew stronger. Every exit had been blocked, making it impossible to leave the house. What did he think would happen to her? If what he said was true and her power was unleashed after last night, she would be less vulnerable. Having nothing else but time on her hands, she explored the house, hoping to find more of him.

The winding staircase looked ancient with its carvings on the mahogany spindles, the hand railing broad and curved to fit her hand as she held onto it. The barren walls were neutral in color and personality. Three large columns divided the living room from the large dining area. The fireplace's face, done in rich metallic browns, was easily seen from all areas.

The burning sensation clawed her insides, reminding her of the earlier shower incident, but she was not thinking of leaving him. A panic began building in the pit of her stomach.

Was he leaving her?

The memory of him holding her tightly to him, fighting to unleash her true source of power, gave a different message. If he refused her leaving, he wasn't about to leave her behind. He had accepted family duty and had taken on the danger stalking her. Protective. Slightly domineering.

He had chosen to be hers forever.

Restless, she paced the front of the fireplace and glanced at her watch. Without thinking about, she waved her hand and the fireplace lit up. He had been gone for more than five hours. She ran upstairs and pulled the dresser open where Dante had placed her grandmother's crystal. Slipping it around her neck, she felt something was wrong that she could not put a name to.

She missed the heat of his eyes.

Ached for the touch of his hands.

Wanted the sweet taste of his lips.

Sighing, she knew she was gone in more ways than one. She was missing Dante, period. Lost in thought, she missed her step, reach for the railing, but it was too late and found herself sailing to the marble floor. Below a hot white substance, glittering, began rising, until she was surrounded, safely carrying her to her landing, refusing to be shaken off as she walked quickly to towards the couch. She needed to sit down.

The fire roared in the hearth as she took a seat and looked toward the landing from where she taken a dive. The railing was in place and stood high enough that it was nearly impossible to clear without hitting her body on it as she had sailed over it.

She should not have fallen, so what had tripped her?

A small, black puff dust ball floated in front of her, into the fireplace, and up the chimney.

A man who did not employ housekeepers for such a large home only had to snap his fingers and it would remain dust free. The black dust ball's path came from high above. Her eyes checked the walls and corners for traces of cobwebs or soot escaping the fireplace.

None were visible.

Casting her eyes back at the flames, she thought of Dante. A man who was made of stone and still had enough fire to melt her soul. The flames flickered, casting a trail of light as tiny puffs of black dust trickled to the floor and rolled like tumbleweeds in a ghost town towards the couch. The black puffs continued to fall, surrounding the couch. Raising her feet off the floor, she followed the trail and her heart raced. Forcing herself to stay still and look as though she were unaware of the falling darkness, she laid back on the couch, stretching her body full length. She placed her hands behind her head and closed her eyes enough to hide their true intent.

Through these hooded eyes, she watched the falling black puffs, trying to discern their origination. If Dante's seals weren't letting her out, how were they getting in? Out of the corner of her eye, several of the puffs, as if in slow motion, swept into the fire, pointing out a trail of her only escape.

A portal through the fireplace.

Unsure of who or what had invaded the house, she had to channel her energy and seek the sight within her, allowing the glittery white substance to soak into her soul. It was difficult seeing through the fuzziness of her newly unleashed powers, but she forced herself not to think or feel and continued to lay there with her eyes closed, giving semblance to sleeping. She could feel her energy building into a power wave. There was nothing left to do but let it take over.

Black soon faded into light.

Her sight showed her the fireplace, the columns, the dining room table, stairway, and the black particles falling from the ceiling. Shadows moved on the walls.

Terror squeezed the air out of her lungs.

The ceiling was coated in a thick mass of black clouds.

She begged her soul to let her transform and escape through the portal left unsealed.

Her soul demanded she rely on instincts and her energy.

She knew it was right and forced her body to relax. Something was wrong if the darkness had found them.

Her attacker had found her.

Dante had not returned, which meant she was on her own.

"Hello, Cat." David blocked her only exit. "Long time."

She turned on her side, crooked her arm, and laid her head in the palm of her hand. "David." She watched carefully, remembering well the quiet before the storms.

"You could have had it all. I would've given you anything."

"Blood? Death screams? Terror?" She couldn't help but laugh, knowing it might infuriate him. "Most men think of diamonds or a trip."

Her energy raged inside, preparing for battle.

She just wished it would share the plan with her.

Her soul warned to tread lightly. Someone else was coming near.

"How did you get in here?" she asked, sitting up and waving her hand for a glass of wine for herself and a Scotch for him. She saw his appreciation and acknowledgment of her newly formed skills.

David twirled the amber liquid in his glass, studying it for brief seconds as if he were trying to read her mind. "I grabbed a ride. I have waited a long time to have you fighting by my side, and I don't care if you've given yourself to him. He did me a favor. I would much rather have an experienced woman in my bed. Though Dante was given this opportunity, I look forward to making sure you submit to me." David took a drink and it went from his hand to the mantle. "I really do hate to break bad news to you. Believe me, I never want to extinguish the light in your eyes, but we need to move on to the future as my wife."

Her soul nearly leapt to fire at him, but knew she was not strong enough. This time she demanded it heel. "You killed him." Dante's soul was quiet but not dead. He was still alive, she could feel it in her heart and soul. Buying time was a must. "I have just begun to learn new skills. More by accident than knowledge."

The burning in the heart of her soul came back and it was stronger. Happier. Confident.

Dante was alive and he was coming for her.

And he was weakened from battle.

The energy within grew excited, warning her not to announce his homecoming. There was another source of emotion she couldn't explain. Partly sad and yet a tinge of jealousy attached to this unnamed source. Her energy flowed in circles, waiting for Dante.

"There's no use hoping. He's dead," David said, walking to her, taking the glass of wine from her hand. He moved it next to the Scotch. "I will go easy on you if you come willingly. It is your choice. Choose now."

Hell would freeze over before she went willingly with him, but she had to buy time. She hoped Dante would understand. Bowing her head, she nodded. Dante would not enter David's way. Dante was not an exhibitionist.

David hooked his finger under her chin.

She refused to show any sign of fear and lifted her eyes to him.

"I do have to teach you who's master of my world and make sure you understand the consequences of your behavior. You ran from me. He defied me. You consorted with the enemy," David said.

David's anger was not far away. She could feel the nausea and shivers rising as the past memories of the blood running down walls and screams of terror filling the night reverberated in her mind.

"I did not know Dante was your enemy."

Suddenly, her energy roared to life and she knew Dante was in the house.

And he had brought a woman with him.

"Dante, get out here now or I will destroy Cat's soul," David called out without turning his attention away from Cat. He dropped his finger, preparing for battle as he flexed his hands at his side.

Dante stepped out of the shadows into the firelight and let the wall support him. "Let her go, David. You wanted me. Here I am."

Chapter Twenty-seven

David shook his head, surprise replacing his poker face. He looked between Dante and Cat. "You haven't told her."

"Told me what?" Cat asked, forcing herself to stay put and not run to Dante's side.

"I thought you had died," Dante said.

"You mean you hoped I had died and you were secure in your position," David sneered.

Dante moved and David raised his hand towards Cat. Dante's eyes narrowed, but he nodded and stopped.

"We no longer have a world. We are borrowing this world and so there is no need for a king or a ruler. Their ways are different than ours." *Cat, has he hurt you?*

No. Cat wanted to touch him to see how badly he was hurt.

"I'm surprised you are not dead. Your soul was pierced to the core," David taunted.

Cat lost her breath and almost passed out, remembering Dante's words on how a soul could die.

Dante staggered to catch her before she fell, but Cat righted herself quickly. "I'm still not getting the connection between you two," Cat whispered.

David's smile was slow and pompous. "We are brothers."

"By blood only," Dante said to Cat.

David whipped out a blast when Dante clutched his wound, staggering as the blood seeped between his fingers. Dante went crashing through the banister and lay on the stairs.

Cat's hand flew out before she could stop herself. White light sent David into the face of the fireplace. She ran and leaped into the air, surprising herself and David as she flew, landing at Dante's side.

Dante lay unconscious. Blood poured from his abdomen. A white, glittery substance began trickling out with the blood.

She touched his face, sorrow rushing into her heart, and the tears began falling. "What do I do, Dante? Please tell me," she whispered into his lips as she kissed him, holding her hand over the wound to stop the flow, but it didn't stop.

Surprised David had not attacked, she now knew why.

Dante's soul had been destroyed and there was nothing she could do. She leaned over and hugged him, weeping for a man who was filling to fight for family and for her soul.

She turned her head and peered through the hair covering her face, watching David stand by the fireplace, taking it all in. She knew time was running out for her, too. Whoever had arrived with Dante had left and would not be helping either of them.

Dante had once hinted there was something he had done for Jack's woman, trying to save her, but she had died and Jack had blamed him.

David walked toward the stairway and her.

Cat's soul cried out for more time.

To be with him to the end. To let him know he was not alone in his final hours.

She buried her head in Dante's shoulder and cried. She called out to her soul, begging it do something to help him.

"Cat, get away from him. Now," David ordered, leaping in the air to break them apart.

She would not leave him.

She refused.

He had been there for her when she needed him the most.

It was her turn.

"Cat, I will destroy his body next, if you do not move away from him," David threatened.

She understood enough to know a body did not matter. It was the soul that was important.

But why was David upset when Dante was dying?

Why was he so adamant she move now?

Then she saw why.

A white glitter substance was rising from her body and seeping into his.

Hope flared in her heart. "David, he is in his final moments and you are denying your brother this last piece of humanity? I will go with you willingly if you grant me a few more moments."

David landed at the foot of the stairs. "No. Move away or I will move you myself."

Cat saw the evil in David's eyes. There was no way David would grant enough time for this glittery substance to transfer to Dante's soul. She would hurry the process the only way she knew how. She held out her hand and an object appeared.

"No!" David roared, leaping to take it from her. He sent a power blast toward the knife she held.

"No!" a woman screamed.

Shock registered on Cat's face. The woman had not left as she'd thought, but there was no time to ask questions.

She sat up, looked directly into David's horrified eyes, and plunged the knife into her soul.

David screamed obscenities, blasting waves of power all around.

The woman pulled Cat's shoulders back to observe the wound. Cat shrugged her away, warning she would summon everything to attack. The woman conceded and stepped back as Cat slid the knife out and leaned over Dante.

Glittery substance no longer came from her skin. It surrounded them as white light poured from her soul into Dante's wound.

She could hear the woman crying quietly behind her. Could hear David destroying this home. Could hear her heart beat slowing. Could hear the quick intake of Dante's breath of new life.

She knew she was dying and wanted to hear his voice one more time.

In the distance, before Cat passed out, a woman cried out and another man joined them saying, "Katrina, I got here as fast as I could. What's wrong?"

Chapter Twenty-eight

Jack found Katrina gone when he had awakened that morning. He had not been able to get over the fact they had joined after all these years. So when he received Katrina's message, he eagerly followed her invitation. Finding no seals or traps, he quietly entered through the second floor.

He could smell death. Smell the scent of his brother's insanity in this.

Heard his beloved's grief as a lunatic raged near her.

This was a man Jack had never seen, but his instincts warred. This raging man was the man his brother had hired. Jack understood now. His brother had written a clause that Jack would be Lycon's toy forever and completely—*if* Jack were unable to fulfill his contract.

Jack would not let that happen. Invisibility was a skill he'd come to rely on many a time. He had a duty as a husband to the woman he'd recently joined and as a businessman. With quiet stealth, he stole past Katrina, knowing full well by the slight lifting of her shoulders that she was well aware he was in the room, but he couldn't take that chance of being seen.

Not just yet.

Jack flew into the air and fired an attack on David.

David returned fire, finding nothing to attack. He stood in the center of the room, his hands aimed for a fight he could not see as he moved his body around one-hundred-eighty degrees.

Jack hovered above him, wanting to torture this man on so many levels, but he dare not take the chance of his beloved being destroyed again or being held by Lycon for eternity.

Jack descended in front of David as David stood still. Jack's hand formed a claw and held it at David's soul. From the corner of his eye, he saw Katrina look their way, waiting. Jack summoned his power to the brink and waited until it built to its highest form of destruction and fired. David leaped back from the blast as if he had sensed his coming death, twisting but not escaping the mutilation.

David fired at the stairway.

Jack speared to the ceiling to stop it, but Katrina threw up a shield, protecting them. Katrina walked through the shield and began firing at David. Jack joined Katrina from behind.

David tossed out fireballs, alternating with each hand, before raising his fist to the ceiling and pulling.

The black mass simmering above dropped.

Jack was next to Katrina in a heartbeat and held her close, shielding them both as he blew the black mass into the chimney. When the room cleared, David was gone.

Katrina sank into Jack's arms. "I wasn't sure you had received my message."

Jack said nothing for a moment, enjoying his beloved in his arms once again. "Nothing like joining and skipping out in the morning," he said with a bit of humor laced in his voice. "Is that what the lasses do these days? Thank heaven I don't have a daughter or I would be killing every last man in this world."

His Katrina was scaring him the way she wasn't responding.

Chapter Twenty-nine

"Uh, Jack—" Katrina hesitated. "There's something I've been meaning to talk to you about."

"Another trait that never goes out of style," Jack laughed with irony. "They either want to talk about something you've done or they accidentally let your horse run off." He was in a good mood. The contract was still his and in good standing as Cat had died of her own hand and not David's.

"What is it, my beloved?" he asked when she wouldn't stop crying. It was killing him to see her like this; he had forgotten what it did to his heart.

It made him feel all over again.

"Talk to me," he whispered.

"We had a daughter, Jack," she said through tears. "I was on my way to find you to tell about her, but when I arrived, I was told your soul had died. You were never coming back. Then my stalker was back, and I had to leave her with someone. My mother. It was safer for our daughter to think I was dead."

Jack's heart dropped at the words. He was a father. They had a daughter together. "Where is she?" Then it dawned on him, she had used the word "had." "Where is she?"

Katrina started crying and pointed to the stairway, hiding her head in his chest. "I finally found her again, only to lose her a second time. Our daughter joined Dante, the man you tried to kill. Who wants him dead, Jack? Who?"

A murderous rage built up inside of Jack as he thought of all the mind games Lycon played with everyone. Lycon led him to believe Cat was an intricate part of the new world destroying them. When Jack confronted Lycon days ago, Lycon's traitorous smile acknowledged the birth as his own, knowing Jack would want to make sure Cat never survived.

He saw his daughter and son-in-law dead. They had died to save each other and all because of him and Lycon. He couldn't imagine the satisfaction Lycon would get from Jack killing his own flesh and blood.

"Does Lycon know you are alive?" he asked.

Katrina shook her head. "He was the one who stalked me. He wanted me to join with him, and when I refused, he sought revenge and mutilated my soul. Someone pieced my soul together. To this day, I don't know who it was."

"I don't want Lycon finding out that I know of Cat's true birth. It will protect her."

"She's dead. Her soul is drained from her body."

"I have heard stories of parents raising their children's souls from the dead and using their spouse's soul."

"But Dante's dead."

"No, I'm not."

Jack scowled and Katrina thumped him on the shoulder, shaking her head.

"Well," Jack defended himself, not quite used to the fact he had a daughter, much less a son-in-law. Hoping he could kill him, he asked, "Did you defile her before joining?"

Dante smirked. "No. We did that before you came. No pun intended."

Jack's expression zeroed on Katrina, who took it head on. "You told him?"

"Well, it was the only way you and I could save our daughter, his wife, from death."

"You used me and walked away? You have learned too many ways not of our kind," Jack said.

"And killing is?" Katrina rounded back.

"She has a point." Dante held his cat. "If what you said earlier is true, and she can be healed by all of us, then I will have the pleasure of spanking your daughter for giving her life for me."

Jack fought hard not curse in front of Katrina. He was having a hard enough time as it was learning he had been trying to kill his own daughter.

Jack cleared his throat, not wishing to embarrass himself by any display of emotion.

A weakness he could not afford.

Jack took Katrina by the hand and walked to Cat.

Dante placed his hands over Cat's soul. Jack held his hands over her mind. And Katrina touched Cat's heart with her fingertips.

They called upon their souls, their energy.

Glitter white substance glowed as it dripped from their hands into Cat's body.

Cat, please live. There are two people who want to meet you. Please. I have come to love you as no other. You are the only woman of my life. My soul has found its match. Dante leaned forward and kissed Cat on the lips.

Color seeped into Cat's cheeks and lips. Her chest moved slightly and lurched up as she inhaled a deep breath. Her eyes slammed open in terror, remembering.

"It's okay, my little cat. I am alive and well. Thanks to you, but you are in trouble for taking your life. Never do that again," Dante warned. "I love you."

Cat slid her fingertips across the strong jaw line. "I am in love with you. A man whose strength I admire and depend on."

"For the love of—"

"Jack!" Katrina admonished playfully. "Forgive your father, for he is just getting used to the idea of being a father the first time around." All three sets of eyes flanked her statement. "What? You didn't think my body had stopped procreating? It was the chance we had taken in joining. In a matter of months, you will be a father. Another daughter will join us."

Dante quelled the questions rising to Cat's lips. "I will explain later. Now you must rest. Then we will make up for lost time." Dante's expression said he was going to enjoy antagonizing Jack.

"I have business to tend to. Katrina, are you ready?" Katrina accepted his hand and stood, joining Jack. "We have lost time to make up to make up for, also."

Jack had no idea how the hell he was going to play this hand out, but he would do whatever he needed to stay whole and protect his family while keeping it all from Lycon's reach. He snapped his fingers, yanking his beloved in his arms and kissing her madly as they vanished.

Chapter Thirty

Cat would never understand in a million years how a year could totally transform one's life to this. Her family certainly gave new definition to dysfunctional. She laughed at Dante as he read her mind.

He resorted to their traditional way of telepathy. *Soon we will go visit my parents.*

They're still alive?

She shrieked with laughter as he hooked his hand around her neck and drew her close, kissing her soundly and thoroughly, while his other hand tucked her hips into his, to see what he had in mind.

I love you, Dante. This isn't over is it?

It will never be over for our kind. Not with a man like Lycon and his followers. Hopefully, Jack will have changed sides. Now let's focus on our next flight.

Cat was ready to fly and didn't mind having a parachute as they came down. Dante was all she needed.

I love you, Cat. Don't ever stop loving me. I couldn't bear to be without you.

*

Lycon paced the floor, waiting as Jack finished his report on David attacking Cat and Dante. He kept Katrina and the knowledge Cat was his daughter out of the picture. Jack explained Dante had joined with Cat, their power stronger than ever, outranking his.

God help him if Lycon didn't believe him.

Lycon stared hard at Jack, drilling his black, evil eyes, hoping for a reason to destroy Jack. There was none. Jack could see into Lycon's mind. Lycon thought Jack was telling the truth, but there was a foul scent of betrayal somewhere in between. Lycon was confident the betrayal would surface and was a patient man when it came to sniffing out betrayal.

Jack was better.

He had a family to protect.

A reason to get out of his contract and join the light.

More From This Author

Sweet Revenge by Kay Rogal

http://www.crimsonromance.com/crimson-romance-ebooks/
crimson-romance-book-genres/romance-suspense-novels/
sweet-revenge/

Prologue

Selena Malone sat huddled in a corner, a gun between her knees, ready to protect herself and her team. She needed time to think. Exhaustion had set in from the emotions toiling throughout her mind. Her body needed a release from the pent-up energy of what was to come.

What needed to be done.

She'd seen the warning signs and ignored them. His touch, his smell, his whispered words were so good in a time of darkness. When had she allowed a traitor inside her heart? She didn't have to look at her watch to know she had moments before she would have to run. Her team was in danger, because she had allowed him into heart. And her bed.

When had he turned?

Why had he turned?

Had their love meant anything?

"Selena?"

Damn. She wasn't ready for a lover's lies or confrontations. But she'd learned life did not always give you the time you needed in dealing with the challenges it gave you.

She lifted her head, her hair still covering her face. If he had seen her expression, he would've seen the motto their agents were known for. "Dean."

He was boyishly handsome.

She caught a glimpse of the coolness in his blue eyes, his stance too casual. When he tried too hard to be nonchalant, he was ready to kill.

"Where's your backup?" he asked.

"Does it matter?"

He smiled a lover's smile. "I want my woman protected."

I bet, she thought. "Tell me it's not true."

"What?"

"Dammit, Dean, don't play with me. It's not the day or time," she said, leaning forward, her hair covering the gun and her hands.

He laughed. "Ahhhh ... we can take care of that right here."

First rule of thumb ... Don't patronize a woman.

"They say you're a turncoat," she said, moving her thumb in place.

"I would never turn on my team."

Second rule of thumb ... Don't lie to a woman.

"How else would Donovan's men have known about Sean and Adam? They were undercover for three years, wanting Donovan stopped before any more lives were destroyed. They were within a week of taking Donovan out and he never suspected."

Dean's mouth curved into a lover's smile. "I lost my wife to this job. She didn't like it when I disappeared all the time."

The third, and most important, rule of thumb ... Don't ever use a girl to create a cat fight.

Selena stood up with one jump, her gun at her leg. She approached him with a smile that made promises burn out of control. "What was the last straw in turning?"

She advanced and when she was a kiss away, she stood on her toes, waiting.

"You were the deciding factor."

Her lips touched his. "How?"

"Wouldn't you like to know?" He smiled into the kiss.

She kissed him for old time's sake, feeling nothing but a lover's betrayal. "Not really." She tucked her arm into his chest. "A part of me will miss you, though."

"Miss me? You can't get rid of me. I've been prom— "

He reeled back and blood poured from his head as he went down. It wasn't her shot. She looked around, seeing nothing, hearing nothing. Silencer. The men had promised her she had this one all alone. Who had taken the head shot?

It was time to leave this scene. She needed laughter, a little sunshine, and just plain good folks. Some sense of a normal life before it was too late.

And a decent cup of coffee.

Chapter One

Puffs of smoke sailed across the room. Danten paced the floor, rolling the cigar between his thumb and fingers before lifting it to his mouth. He paused.

"Did you find her?" Danten finally asked.

The seasoned investigator, who called himself Jones, waved the smoke away.

"She's covered her trail completely, sir. No credit card, phone, or any other kind of data exists. Even her comrades — "

"Former comrades," Danten said quietly.

"Even they haven't seen her."

"Not that they would want to after her former lover turned against his own team. She had guts wanting to finish him off face-to-face." Danten puffed on his cigar a few more times and went back to rolling it between his fingers, knowing she hadn't pulled the trigger. But then ... no one knew who had but him. "When she walked out on the mission, it was the final straw. They could understand being taken in by a lover, but not a comrade leaving them high and dry in a mission." He knew the silent code of honor.

She would be on her own.

Jones stepped forward slightly, hesitating. "Why look her up after all this time?"

"Because she can take care of her sister's debt."

"But you're—"

Danten snuffed out his cigar back and forth with gentle motions. He laid the cigar down and waited. "Do you have any other leads?"

Jones hesitated again. Was he having second thoughts? "No. I'll let you know as soon as I receive any info."

"I see." Danten's eyes narrowed, but he nodded and smiled. As Jones turned away, he asked, "Don't you want your other half of the fee?"

There was the slightest pause, but Jones continued out the door. "No. I can get it when you get the rest of your information."

"Our deal was paid in full regardless of the outcome as long you uncovered every nook and cranny."

"I did."

"I have your money."

Danten had picked the investigator for the greedy soul he possessed. And his refusal of the money meant he was letting his scruples get in the way of doing the job. Danten opened his desk drawer — and in a moment it was over.

Danten didn't wait for the investigator's last breath before reaching inside the man's jacket and pulling out the envelope he found there. He ripped the envelope open. Just as he suspected, Jones had found her.

Sliding the envelope and its contents into his briefcase, he snapped the locks into place. A few well-placed leads under the right noses and he would take it from there.

In time, Selena would pay her sister's debt.

In the mood for more Crimson Romance? Check out *Coming Home* by Christine S. Feldman at *CrimsonRomance.com*.